New Fiction

TWISTING TALES

Edited by

Chiara Cervasio

First published in Great Britain in 2004 by
NEW FICTION
Remus House,
Coltsfoot Drive,
Peterborough, PE2 9JX
Telephone (01733) 898101
Fax (01733) 313524

SB ISBN 1 85929 112 0

FOREWORD

When 'New Fiction' ceased publishing there was much wailing and gnashing of teeth, the showcase for the short story had offered an opportunity for practitioners of the craft to demonstrate their talent.

Phoenix-like from the ashes, 'New Fiction' has risen with the sole purpose of bringing forth new and exciting short stories from new and exciting writers.

The art of the short story writer has been practised from ancient days, with many gifted writers producing small, but hauntingly memorable stories that linger in the imagination.

I believe this selection of stories will leave echoes in your mind for many days. Read on and enjoy the pleasure of that most perfect form of literature, the short story.

Parvus Est Bellus.

CONTENTS

SHERLOCK'S LAST CASE
Gwen Liddy

It had been a particularly brutal murder.

Raymond 'Sherlock' Selby had felt physically sick at the gruesome sight of the blood spattered corpse. Selby had seen many such sights, some even more gruesome, but none had affected him quite this way before. He decided that this would be his last case and for that reason he was determined to bring it to a speedy and successful conclusion, thus ending his career on a high note.

Selby had earned the nickname 'Sherlock' due to his ability to solve even the most bafflingly complex of murders and for his penchant for Sherlock Holmes stories.

Selby, a widower living alone, had for long dreamed of a Caribbean cruise now, he decided, was the time to take early retirement and go off on his cruise.

However he must first turn his attention to the matter in hand. The body of a farmer, Bill Bryson, aged thirty-nine, owner of Oak Tree Farm, situated a mile or so from the Devon village of Cheriton, had been found that morning in a Dutch barn with a pitchfork embedded in his back. The left prong of the fork had gone right through his body pinning him to the floor and smashing his fob watch; setting the time of the murder at five minutes past ten. The farmer had last been seen drinking in the village inn, the 'Farmer's Rest', just after nine o'clock that evening. He had left alone to cycle back to his farm.

The doctor's preliminary report was that death had been instantaneous due to damage to the left ventricle and pulmonary veins. Forensic had not come up with any useful evidence. The pitchfork had been widely used and showed too many fingerprints to be conclusive. Bryson had in his possession, when found, a considerable amount of money which ruled out robbery as the motive for the murder.

There were five people, five suspects, who at sometime or other had harboured a grudge against Bryson but all had given reasonable explanations as to where they were at the time of the murder. One of them was obviously lying but which one?

The murder team of ten had gathered in the large dining room of the farm house and were now seated around the refectory table. On a blackboard in a corner of the room had been pinned a blown-up photograph of the corpse and beneath it photos of the five suspects.

Selby addressed the team. 'Well gentlemen we have all the evidence, the statements, forensic and pathologist reports now it is up to us to find the guilty person.'

First suspect was Robert Bryson, twenty-nine, the farmer's only son. Motive for murder - financial gain.

Robert Bryson was something of a wastrel. He was rarely seen at the farm but chose to spend most of his time in the fleshpots of London. He had however recently come to stay in Cheriton village to escape the attentions of numerous debt collectors who were pursuing him for non-payment of gambling debts amounting to thousands of pounds.

His father refused to help him out by giving him money, saying that he had brought it on himself and must sort out his own problems.

Robert's alibi was that he had spent the evening in the town of Tiverton and returned to the village on the nine-twenty branch line train, which should have reached Cheriton Halt at nine-forty but due to a signal failure it had not reached Cheriton until ten-fifteen, a fact confirmed by the railway staff.

He now stood to inherit his father's estate, enough to settle his debts many times over.

Robert Bryson was a very likely suspect.

Second suspect was John Hurly, aged forty-five, owner of an adjoining farm. Motive for murder - a border dispute.

Hurly had been engaged in a bitter, long running, dispute with Bryson over a tract of land which both said was their property. Hurly had erected a fence around the disputed area which Bryson had promptly torn down. The matter was now in the hands of solicitors and an outcome was awaited. There was no love lost between the two men. On the night of the murder there had been strong words exchanged between them in the bar of the 'Farmer's Rest'.

Hurly had left the inn just after Bryson and gone back to his farm.

The question was did this grievance cause him enough anger to commit murder?

Third suspect was Sammy Willerby, aged twenty-two a farm hand at Oak Tree Farm. Motive for murder - angst.

Sammy was something of a simpleton, easily taken in and the butt of much, often cruel, ribbing which for most part he took in good humour. However, on the day before the murder Jack Tenby, another farm worker had sent him to the village to purchase a 'left-handed' spanner. Knowing Tenby to be left-handed Sammy had set off on his fool's errand and spent much of the morning going from shop to shop, much to the amusement of the shopkeepers.

When Sammy realised that he had been taken in yet again he reacted with uncharacteristic anger, he had walked furiously away from the farm and had not been seen again that day.

Could his angst have boiled over to such an extent that he had taken it out on Bryson? Not very likely but nevertheless he remained a suspect.

Number four suspect was Colin Smith, aged twenty-two, living in a tied cottage on the edge of the farm. Motive for murder - crime passionel.

Colin had married a local girl, Betty, an attractive twenty-year-old blonde. Bill Bryson had taken quite a shine to her, his attentions not always discouraged by Betty, and it was known that when Jack was away and Bryson was working near the cottage he would call in to take his mid-morning break there where, so it was rumoured, he would get considerably more than a cup of cocoa.

If Colin knew what was going on he ignored it probably because to do otherwise he would risk losing the tied cottage.

But, did pride and anger cause him to commit murder? It was a strong possibility.

The fifth and final suspect was Jack Tenby, aged thirty-five. Motive for murder - fraud.

Tenby was Bryson's chargehand. A good all round and willing worker. He lived in a flat by the village green, easy going and popular among the village residents. Bryson had come to rely upon him for, since the death of his, Bryson's, wife a few years ago Tenby had taken on much of the paperwork today's farming entails. He kept the accounts and filled in numerous government forms at which Bryson himself was quite hopeless.

But unbeknown to Bryson Jack Tenby had for sometime been 'fiddling the figures'. He had set up a bogus company, 'C & D Feed Company', and had defrauded his employer of several thousands of pounds by paying small but significant sums of money into his bogus account.

Bryson, although not suspecting Tenby of any impropriety, had been for sometime concerned that profits from the farm were not as good as they should be. He told Jack that he was going to bring in a chartered accountant to examine the books and see what savings could be made.

Tenby was dismayed. He knew that once the accountant ran his eagle eye over the books his deceit would be revealed and he faced at least the sack and possibly a prison sentence. He knew he must avoid the accountant's inspection at all costs. For that reason did he kill Bryson?

Tenby's alibi was that on the evening of the murder he too had gone to Tiverton to see a film at the Regal Cinema. By way of proof he produced his half of the admission ticket. He returned to Cheriton on the nine-twenty train and was home just in time to see the start of the ten o'clock news on ITV. Was he telling the truth?

Raymond 'Sherlock' Selby was convinced he knew who the guilty party was, he wondered if the team had come to the same conclusion. The team embarked on a long and noisy discussion, eventually coming to the conclusion that suspect number one was the murderer on account that he had the most to gain from his father's untimely end. Robert Bryson now stood to inherit the entire farm which, when sold, would make him richer by at least half a million pounds, enough to clear all his gambling debts and finance his wasteful gambling habits for a long time to come.

With this 'Sherlock' did not agree. 'You are missing,' he said, 'two vital clues. Look closely at the photo of the corpse and the pathologist report. Bryson was attacked from behind. Only one prong of the fork, the left one, has completely penetrated the body which indicates a left bias, therefore the assailant is cack-handed. We know from the business of the spanner that Tenby is left-handed which in itself is not conclusive but a closer look at his alibi shows that he is undoubtedly lying.

He said that he returned to Tiverton by the nine-twenty train and was indoors by ten o'clock but we know from a previous statement that that train did not reach Cheriton Halt until ten-fifteen. Tenby was not on that train. He killed Bryson to prevent an accountant's inspection of the books. Do you agree?'

Reluctant though they were to admit that their theory was wrong they had to agree with Selby's deductions.

'Then let's find out if I am right,' Selby said, 'call in the suspects.'

The five suspects came in and arranged themselves by the board.

'We think,' Selby said, 'that the murderer is you Jack Tenby.'

Tenby stepped forward grinning. 'Yes guv,' he said, 'it was me. I am your man.'

The team sat back laughing and gave Selby a ripple of applause. These 'murder weekends' were to Raymond Selby, a bank manager by profession, a great and relaxing way of spending his time away from the bank's business of accounts, overdrafts, mortgages. Now at sixty-three it was time to take early retirement and go off on his long dreamed of cruise. He had earned it.

Three months or so later, relaxing on a sunbed on the 'Ocean Queen' beneath an azure Caribbean sky, a large iced drink to hand, engrossed in his favourite Sherlock Holmes story Raymond Selby felt very content. The cruise was everything he had imagined it would be.

Long relaxing days sunbathing, good food, charming company, plenty of inboard entertainments, Raymond could not have wished for a better start to his retirement.

Today was to be one of the highlights of the cruise, the ship would shortly be anchored off Nassau, the capital of the Bahama islands. A tour of the capital had been arranged followed by a barbecue on Paradise Beach to which Selby was much looking forward to.

A nearby tannoy suddenly came to life. 'Attention,' came a voice, 'due to unforeseen circumstances the tour of Nassau and the barbecue have been cancelled. A further announcement will be made shortly. All passengers are requested to remain in or near their cabins.'

Raymond felt a pang of disappointment he had been looking forward to Nassau and the chance to buy souvenirs.

A steward was hovering close by.

'Why,' Selby asked him, 'have they cancelled the tour?'

'Well,' the steward said, 'I don't think there is any harm in my saying, you will know soon enough. This morning the body of a steward was found in a store room with a cook's knife in his back. The police will want to question everyone.'

Raymond Selby (Sherlock) closed his book, rose, took a long sip of his iced drink.

It was time once again to put on the thinking cap, or as Hercule Poirot would put it, more eloquently, time to exercise the little grey cells - only this time it would be for real.

THE INTRUDER
Ann Blair

One ray of sunshine fell onto the stone floor. A small ray of hope in a world gone crazy. The nightmare continued as every day passed, when a second seemed as long as an hour. The stark cold walls were somehow in keeping with the hopelessness that engulfed Sam. How much longer would the torture continue? The endless sleepless nights and the awful stench of this place that would stay with her forever. One mistake, one foolish act and her life may as well be over. Didn't anyone understand she hadn't meant to hurt anyone, least of all him? It had been a terrible accident that wasn't anyone's fault. A case of being in the wrong place at the wrong time when fate had conspired against her.

Sam's stomach clenched as she heard heavy footsteps approaching, although she wanted it all to be over, she was dreading the outcome. Disappointment and pure relief were the twin emotions Sam wrestled with when the footsteps went by her door. She sank down on the hard bench of a bed and silently offered a prayer that somehow she'd have the strength to get through the rest of this terrible ordeal. She mustn't cry. She mustn't give in. Whatever happened today, Sam wanted to keep some dignity. More footsteps, a key in the door and Sam glanced up at the bars on the window. Whatever the verdict was, she knew she would remain in hell for at least the foreseeable future. Bracing herself she rose to her feet and faced her defence lawyer.

'It won't be long now, I just came to see if you were holding up.' Jake Drummond said kindly.

Sam nodded and sat back down on the bed before she gratefully took the tea he had brought her. Sipping the hot liquid Sam thought back to the night she'd had the argument with Tony, and the chain of events that had culminated in her being charged.

She and Tony had been living together for a year and Sam had prepared a special meal to celebrate their anniversary. They had planned to get married the following spring, but when Tony finally arrived home that evening, Sam was so furious with him that she told him the wedding was off, amongst quite a few other things. He'd forgotten to tell her he was working late and hadn't even bothered to ring. Sam hadn't had a very good day at work, she was tired and thoroughly fed up, the meal was ruined, the evening spoilt and she felt taken for granted. Tony's offer to take her out for dinner the following night didn't appease Sam's ill humour in the slightest, and in the end she flounced out of the flat and drove over to her parents' house. They were on holiday in Spain at the time, and with her brother being away in the army, Sam had the house to herself and a place to escape from Tony. She opened the door to the darkened house and disenabled the burglar alarm. Putting her handbag on the kitchen table she filled the kettle and switched it on before she sat down. Sam was determined to teach Tony a lesson. They hadn't spent a night apart since they had moved in together, but he could be very thoughtless at times. The trouble was that Sam loved him so much she couldn't stay angry with him for long, and she was already beginning to regret her actions, once she started to calm down. She hadn't really meant what she'd said, in fact she realised she had rather over reacted, and Sam was the first to admit that she could be hot headed at times. She decided that once she'd finished her tea she would go home and make up with Tony, who would be getting worried about her by now.

Sam popped up to the bathroom to wash her tearstained face, not bothering to put on the light in the hallway. The moon shining in through the landing window illuminated the stairs sufficiently and Sam was preoccupied with thoughts of what she was going to say to Tony. She splashed cold water on her face, patted it dry and then she thought she heard muffled sounds coming from below. Sam stood very still, straining her ears until she heard something being knocked over. Sam froze and began to feel frightened, there was someone else in the house and it had to be an intruder. She remembered her mother mentioning a spate of burglaries when they'd last spoken on the phone and Sam wasn't at all sure if she'd closed the front door properly after she'd disenabled the alarm. She hurriedly flicked off the bathroom light and stood petrified at the top of the stairs. Her throat was dry, her legs were shaking and she thought her heart would explode. Then she saw a shadowy figure lurching into the hall. Sam was absolutely terrified; she shook from head to toe. Her mobile phone was in her bag in the kitchen and her parents' landline was downstairs in the hall. She couldn't even phone for help. She was completely on her own.

Sam shrank back against the landing wall as the intruder made for the stairs. The moon had gone behind a cloud but she could still make out his bulky form. He was tall, much taller than she was and probably high on drugs. He stumbled once or twice as he slowly climbed the stairs, and Sam was in fear of her life. She knew it was now or never as he neared the top and summoning all her courage, Sam put her head down and charged at him, pushing with all her might. She knocked him completely off balance and he fell backwards, his head hitting each stair with a sickening thud, until he ended up in a crumpled heap at the foot of the staircase. With a strangled sob Sam hurried down after him and gingerly stepped over his prostrate form. She couldn't bear to look at him as she phoned the police and then she sat huddled in a chair until the patrol car arrived. Sam went into shock when she was told that she'd killed him and by the time she was taken to the police station she was beside herself with grief.

Sam stood up and paced her cell restlessly; she needed Tony to be with her right now. He was her strength and he'd been wonderful these last few weeks, but now it was up to the jury. Jake squeezed Sam's shoulder reassuringly when at last she was called, and in a trance-like state she walked back into court. She glanced over to where her parents were sitting, but they had their eyes to the floor. The sadness etched on their faces was heartbreaking for Sam to see.

I didn't know, she wanted to scream. *No one told me he was home on leave and out drinking with his friends that evening.* Sam no longer cared what happened to her. She knew that as long as they both lived, her mother and father would never really forgive her. And Sam would never forgive herself for killing her younger brother.

JACOB'S DREAM
David Heaver

November 2002

The afternoon sun made Sam drowsy as he lolled contentedly aboard his 41ft cruiser 'Jacob's Dream', the fishing line dangling flaccidly in the warm waters of the Caribbean, a bottle of Corona Extra beside his seat. With Jacob and Lilly gone, he'd decided to live his dream now, while he had the chance. He pulled on the cold beer; yes this was the life.

May 2001

Jacob had seen it all: tourists, locals, drunks and lovers; nothing fazed him. He sat patiently waiting for the lights to change; his large leathery hands the colour of mahogany drumming the steering wheel in time with Muddy Waters' classic 'Mannish Boy' emanating from the radio.

A few more months and he would have saved enough money to live his dream; to do what he had been planning since Veronica left him. Fifteen years it had taken to be sure he could escape this crazy city and live the life he deserved. He didn't need another woman in his life, that was the last thing he wanted. No, his dream was simple: a boat, a small place at the beach and to fish quietly under the warm Caribbean sun. The toothy smile split his face as he pictured the scene in his mind. Yes, this was his payback for long winters as a New York cabbie.

The following weekend was not one for driving his cab however. This weekend was to indulge his other passion in life, one final pilgrimage to Chicago for the annual Blues Festival. He liked Chicago in the summer when it was warm. It may be the Windy City in those arctic winter months but in the early summer sunshine it was such a great place, full of life and music. With the lakeside skyline proudly dominated by the gleaming black monoliths of the Sears Tower and the John Hancock Observatory, Chicago never failed to impress.

Sam Prince was browsing in a downtown Chicago bookshop. Dressed in black, wearing make-up and looking rather menacing, he attracted the attention of the store owner who watched him suspiciously on the video monitor. As Jacob entered, the opening door agitated a small wind-chime dangling above it. A copy of 'Fishing The Caribbean' in the window had commanded his attention on his way back to the festival in Grant Park.

'Hi there, how are you today?' enquired the owner.

'Good thanks,' replied Jacob, 'that fishing book you have in the window . . .'

'Good choice Sir,' he answered, adding caustically, 'over there, near Count Dracula,' indicating towards Sam with a nod of the head.

'Fishing the Caribbean; awesome,' commented Sam as they stood side by side. They introduced themselves and Jacob found himself in conversation with the young Goth. Despite his rebellious appearance he seemed like a cool kid, intelligent and unexpectedly interested in Jacob's plans for his 'retirement'. Sam seemed desperate to share his own Caribbean story . . . the words just tumbled from his mouth.

'God knows, I hate winter in this city, it's so damned raw,' he reflected. 'My aunt told me a lot about life on the islands. She lived there before coming here in '66 when she married my uncle. I see her a lot but she fell on hard times when my uncle died and now she lives on the streets for most of the year. During the winter she uses the shelters to avoid the cold, I mean, I guess she must be about 60 now. It's weird but she talks about losing her husband as her 'second bereavement' but she's never talked about the first. But hey, she is always cheerful even if she is a little wacky these days. I envy her freedom and her refusal to conform. My folks have money; Dad's umm, well he's in business, but they're so uptight. They don't like people who 'express their individuality' so I have to stand on my own. So . . . do you know anyone in the Caribbean who could use some help?'

'Maybe,' Jacob frowned . . . something didn't add up.

Jacob decided against buying the book, flashy cover but lacking content. He noticed Sam still being eyed by the store owner, a tall, good looking man with sandy hair and piercing blue 'bedroom eyes'. Jacob decided he didn't like his attitude. *He judges a book by the cover* he thought . . . then smiled as he realised his unintended pun.

Jacob and Sam left the shop together. 'You wanna get a cup of coffee?' Jacob offered in his distinctive New York accent, keen to hear more of the boy's story and with an hour to kill before the music started again down by the lake. Sam liked the old man and gratefully accepted.

They sunk into the comfortable, worn leather armchairs in Starbucks and looked out onto the street scene as they chatted. An old-looking lady ambled past the window and glanced in. Jacob met her eyes and she smiled, pausing for a moment as though there was a glimmer of recognition. He smiled back through the window, the scarlet flower in her hair, her white teeth somehow out of keeping with her otherwise moth-eaten appearance. In that moment she looked so familiar, but he couldn't place her. She strolled off slowly down Washington towards Michigan Avenue, under the 'L', Chicago's elevated rail track and past the CTA Station, her long powder blue skirt swinging like a bell, sweeping the pavement as she went.

Jacob gazed wistfully after her, not hearing what Sam was saying, trying to place the face that had just looked at him and the walk that seemed so familiar.

'Hey man!' The voice shook him back to reality.

'Sorry Sam, what did you say?'

'That was my aunt, the one I told you about. That old lady who looked in was smiling at me.'

Jacob was bewildered, 'She's your aunt? But . . . but she's, well, she's black.'

'Yeah, you see, Uncle Al was my dad's brother, a salesman for the family business who travelled all over the Caribbean. That is where he met my aunt Lilly.'

'Lilly you say?'

'Yeah. They had both loved fishing.'

'Fishing?'

Sam continued with his story . . . 'They spent many weekends together on her small boat, fishing, talking and finally they became lovers. She had been very passionate, you know, in the way that Caribbean girls are. Hey, like I need to tell you, right? Anyway, Uncle Al had never experienced anything like her lust for life so he married her. Of course, returning to Chicago with a black bride in the 1960s was not quite what a respected family had expected or were prepared to tolerate. My grandfather immediately disinherited them both, although Uncle Al was still expected to work for the family firm.

Lilly was a singer; she had a great voice . . . still does. She used to sing in a jazz club owned by a friend of Al's. Uncle Al had continued to travel but on one of his trips to Jamaica in 1976, he was driven off the road by a drunk and was killed. Aunt Lilly was devastated and could no longer work. The family ignored her and soon she lost everything.'

They chatted on through another cup of coffee before saying their farewells and going their separate ways. It had been an interesting meeting but something perplexed Jacob.

Later that afternoon as he stood in Grant Park listening to a performance of 'Sweet Home Chicago' Jacob noticed a couple in front of him. The man was grey-haired but had a young face; his evident lack of rhythm and his pallor suggested he was almost certainly a Brit. His companion was younger, darker-skinned with long black curly hair. She was stylish, pretty and, Jacob couldn't help noticing, had a figure that fitted her jeans to perfection.

But someone else had caught his eye. Standing to the left of the couple was Sam's aunt. Jacob didn't know her as Lilly but he was certain he knew her. As she turned her head to say something to the Englishman it struck him, he knew exactly who she was. Stepping forward he put his hand lightly on her shoulder. 'Martha?' He noticed her scent; not the stench of the streets but a subtle aroma of flowers.

She turned . . . 'Jacob? No, it can't be. Jacob Cabral? Oh my God.'

Lilly, or rather Martha, had been Jacob's first love. As teenagers they had fished from her dad's boat and that is what had sparked his love of fishing and what had prompted his dream to return home. He had always known in his heart that Martha had been the one true love of his life and although he would never admit it, he had secretly hoped that one day they might meet up again. But he never expected it to happen in Chicago.

Over dinner, Martha filled the missing years. She had been heartbroken when Jacob left for New York and she had married Al on the rebound. It was he who had called her Lilly because of her love of flowers. Al was a good man and they had lived happily for the ten years they were married. But Al wasn't Jacob and Martha had always known that there was something missing in her life.

It transpired she did have money; quite a lot in fact, finally paid out by Al's life insurance; uncharacteristically overlooked by the family. She had chosen her life on the street because a home reminded her of what she had lost, and besides, she liked the street people far better than Al's family. Except for Sam of course, he was a good kid. And she hadn't really slept rough in hostels during the winter, but had rented a small room above her old jazz club.

September 2001 . . .

This was it, Jacob's last day at work. The day had dawned bright, a beautiful morning. He'd kissed Martha as she slept serenely and started his final shift early, 4.30am. Tomorrow they would be on the plane home and in three days they would be married. Sam had already gone ahead to make the arrangements. After almost forty years, they were to live out their dream together.

After delivering a few night birds home to their nests, Jacob drove a young couple to JFK to catch the early flight to Denver. It was always worth waiting at the airport for a return fare and sure enough, thirty minutes later, an immaculately dressed businessman climbed in the back and gave an address in lower Manhattan. Traffic was flowing well at this early hour, the air was clear, the morning sun illuminating the New York architecture. Yes, despite its problems, he was going to miss this city.

The sunlight reflected off the magnificent twin towers of the World Trade Centre as sentinel-like against the cloudless blue sky they stood, proudly standing guard across the city. This was a good place to be in a cab; there were always decent fares to be had as New York's commercial centre went about its business. After all, *'The Suits'* were all on expenses so were happy to add a few dollars to the tip as long as they got a receipt.

Jacob found a taxi stand in a street adjacent to the towers and settled back in his seat to wait for his next customer. He wasn't going to chase fares today; he would let them come to him.

The huge explosion made him duck his head instinctively, then nothing, silence. He looked around, then checked his watch. It was 8.48am; the date showed Sept 11. It would take eight seconds before tons of debris from American Airlines Flight 11, striking the North Tower 100 floors above him, crashed down on Jacob and his yellow cab. He was one of the first to die that day. For Jacob there had been no time to fear or be sad or be sorry, his dream was ended in a second.

Martha threw herself under a train three months later.

NINE LIVES
Andy Botterill

He looked at his watch. He was running out of time. He knew he should have left sooner, but something inside him had made him stay. He'd wanted to be the last one. He was always the same. Nothing had changed, even after all these years. He wanted to be the last war reporter out of Saigon.

It was determination like this that had helped make his reputation. It was his willingness to push himself to the far extremities of his own limits, to put his life at risk, time and time again, that had made him one of the most sought-after journalists of his generation. Like a cat, he had nine lives, but had just about used up every one of them. This time his luck was running out.

He'd always had some kind of inner sixth sense that had allowed him to walk the tightrope, to hover over the proverbial precipice, and still escape, but this time he'd left it too late. He was in serious danger and he knew it.

He had been warned: be at the airport by one o'clock at the latest. Be at the airport then and we can still get you out. Leave it later than that and you take your chances. He hadn't listened. It was now two o'clock and he was still stuck in a huge queue of traffic heading towards the airport.

Everyone was going that way it seemed. Everyone wanted to get out. He hadn't anticipated so much traffic. How stupid! He should have done of course. He was a bloody journalist for God's sake. He knew the situation better than anyone else. These people were running for their lives, just like he was. And there were only so many more runs the planes could make.

The 'Cong were already at the edge of the city. It wouldn't be long before they overran it. He had an hour or two at most, an hour or two to get to the airport, get on a plane and get out. He'd never wished to be back home so much in his life. He'd had some narrow escapes in the past. He'd been to just about every trouble spot in the world, Africa, South America, the Middle East, but he'd never felt quite like this. It was partly because he'd allowed himself to become separated from his film crew. That had contributed to the situation he now found himself in. He'd let them leave whilst they still had a chance of finding a plane.

It had been the decent thing to do. They'd been very good to him. He wanted to give them something back, to repay their faith. They had wives, families, back home to think about. They'd stayed as long as they could. It was just without them he suddenly felt terribly alone. Despite the incessant heat, a strange chill went through him. It was as if he somehow knew this time he wasn't coming back. This was it, his last assignment.

He feared what would happen to him if he got left behind. He feared what would happen if he fell into the hands of the 'Cong. Rumours of their cruelty to prisoners was legendary. In fact the atrocities carried out by both sides during this terrible war had been stomach churning. He'd witnessed it, seen it first hand; whole villages laid to waste, women raped, children burned. No one wanted to fall into the hands of the 'Cong. That was why what seemed like the population of the entire city was heading towards the airport with him, with a sense of desperation he'd rarely seen. No one dared be left behind. He was scared he'd be taken for an American. He knew what they thought of Americans and did to them, perhaps with some justification, but he was English. He just hoped they'd know the difference. That was if he didn't get to the airport, if he didn't get on the plane, if he didn't get back to London. He still hoped he just might. There was still that outside chance they might have waited. It had only been an hour, but they wouldn't wait forever.

It was just this bloody traffic jam. He was still stuck in it, and the cars just weren't moving. Horns were beeping, people were shouting and screaming, but nothing was shifting. It was blocked solid. Cars were trying to get out of every side road, but they just couldn't move. It was hopeless. That was when he decided to ditch the truck, just leave it and try to get to the airport by foot. The pavements were as busy as the roads, he found. He tried to push his way through the crowd. Whole families were trying to move with him, clutching hold of a few scant possessions they couldn't bring themselves to leave behind. For his part he still had a camera and a tape recorder. He'd dumped everything else, but he hadn't forgotten he was still a journalist. That was his reason for being there and he'd still document what he could.

The sound of gunfire was getting nearer, although he was aware it had become more sporadic. Resistance to the advance of the 'Cong had now more or less ceased. It was pointless, a lost cause. Like himself, the

'Cong were now more inconvenienced by the number of people on the street than any military opposition they faced.

He decided to take to the back streets. It seemed his best chance. Everything else had failed. After all this time he was still a good half mile from where he needed to be, and time was now really running out, if it hadn't already done so. He just didn't know. That was one of the most terrible things of all. Even if he got there, even if he reached the airport, there was only a small possibility there might still be a plane, a helicopter, something, to take him out.

They were using the runway at the American Embassy. It was the only one left where the pilots could still fly in and out from. Some of the city folk had been camped outside for days trying to get a flight. Luckily, he didn't need to do that. He was a priority case, as a foreign national and as a member of the international press corps, and as such had been assured a seat. He just needed to get there. He'd been told one o'clock, but that time had come and passed. He'd blown it, but he was still trying, now more in desperation than anything else. It was just his instinct to survive that was driving him on. He could have just given up, surrendered, turned himself in, but something inside, something inside wouldn't let him. He had to keep going, whilst there was still hope.

There were now men in uniform on the streets. He didn't know if they were government troops or the dreaded 'Cong. He wasn't going to take any chances, so he double-backed to avoid them, anything to avoid being taken. He was now running. He was now running for his dear life. He was panting, sweating. For the first time, he was really scared. As he ran, he feared a bullet in the back at any moment. He feared the pain of a bullet tearing through his flesh. He feared the sensation of blood seeping through his shirt. He feared death.

He was now at the perimeter gate. In the distance he could make out a small aircraft being boarded. Instinctively he knew it was his. He should have been on the flight, and he would have been, if he hadn't been so bloody late. It was his own stupid fault, and now he was paying the price. As the plane filled up with those privileged enough to have places, stewards and military police battled to keep the rest back.

There was a surge towards the gate and some spilled onto the runway, frightened, desperate. Others were crushed against the huge metal fencing in their bid to reach the plane that would take them to freedom. He knew if he was to get on, he would have to somehow get through them, but there was no chance of that. It was simply mayhem. There were just too many of them. He should have been on that plane. He should have been going home, but instead he'd just have to watch powerless, helpless, as it took off, with him not on it, with him still here, and the Vietcong breathing down his neck. He knew they were there. He could sense them, getting closer and closer. They were now at the top of the road, coming into view, jeeps, tanks, barely 100 yards away, and there was his plane moving onto the runway, starting to gather up speed, but with him not on it.

He watched the aircraft and as he did so he felt his heart sink. This was really it. He'd lost his last chance to get out, and there was no longer anything he could do about it. He was about to be captured, and God knew what fate held in store for him then. To be tortured, murdered? He didn't know. And there was his plane, moving down the runway, about to take off.

He started to look away, to prepare to surrender himself to his captors, when he caught something out of the corner of his eye that made him look back.

A small group of people had somehow got onto the runway and were running towards the plane, causing it to veer off course. In his bid to avoid them, the pilot was getting dangerously close to some outside hangers that bordered the runway. It was hard to watch. Would the pilot be able to straighten the aircraft in time or would he not? It was desperately tight. Suddenly a wing made contact with the hangar wall causing the plane to tilt violently. The pilot battled to get it back on its right path, but it was hopeless. It careered sideways before hurtling into the solid bricks of the hangar wall. There was a dull explosion and the plane burst into flames. It was engulfed in an instant. There was nothing anyone could do. Those on board never stood a chance. They were roasted to death as he, the British journalist, watched in numbed, awful silence. No one could have escaped. It was gut-wrenchingly obvious. The crew and passengers were incinerated in their seats in seconds.

As the flames burned brighter, the stench of burning human flesh began to fill the air and made him want to vomit. Then he was struck by the thought that he should have been with them. He should have been dead also, his flesh and bones melting down to their component parts. He had a strange feeling inside. Suddenly, taking his chances with the 'Cong didn't seem so bad. Better that than being in the twisted wreckage of an aircraft, burning to death. Perhaps fate had intervened on his behalf, he thought. Perhaps it had somehow contrived to save him by making him miss the flight. Perhaps he still had one of his nine lives left, and had just used it.

He now turned to face his captors with more relief than he could have imagined possible only a few seconds earlier, ready to embark on a new chapter in his life. He should have been dead anyway, so anything else now would be a bonus.

SPOOKY OR WHAT?
D P Callaghan

The first time I saw her she was leaning on the stile in the hop pole lane, gazing out over the cornfield. She turned her head and smiled at me over her shoulder, as she did, something flashed between us, I don't know what, something like a memory stirred by a smell of fresh bread or baking. Whatever it was it faded as she turned away.

'Hello, isn't it beautiful?' she gestured to the golden corn moving in the slight breeze like a sunrise on the ocean.

I had just turned fourteen, still immature in many things, and not yet interested enough in boys to seek their company but I did have a love for the countryside. And so I was able to understand her enthusiasm.

'Yes, that's my favourite spot where you're standing. Oh! I'm sorry I didn't mean to be rude.'

I was embarrassed as she moved aside.

'That's OK, there's plenty of room.' She smiled that smile again, and somehow I was drawn to stand beside her, we stood looking out across the field for a long time before speaking.

I was quite comfortable and happy to be there, my tummy began to rumble and she began to laugh quietly. 'It sounds like you're hungry young lady, perhaps you'd better head home for lunch.'

She seemed to know what I was thinking.

As I walked home I turned to thank her for her company, she was not there, I looked along the lane, she was not there, I went back to the stile and saw her way out in the field walking and running fingers through the corn, how did she get out there so quick? I watched, as she seemed to fade into the heat haze over the corn, finally disappearing from sight.

The following day was a school day and I spent most of it thinking about the lady by the stile, tall with blonde hair fading to silver around the temples and piercing blue eyes that could chill as quickly as they warm you.

In a vague sort of way she reminded me of my mother although her clothes where strange to me, she wore a skirt of a fabric I'd never seen, and a blazer type jacket that gave her a secretarial like bearing.

The more I thought about her the more I wanted to see her again, our encounters seemed so dream-like that I began to doubt that they had occurred.

Straight after school I rushed round to the lane, as I approached the corner I was both excited and afraid, excited at the thought of meeting her again and afraid that she would not be there.

I need not have worried, she was standing in the same place, same clothes, same expression of rapt joy at the view in front of her.

Again that smile, 'I'm glad you came.' Her voice was soft, almost wistful. 'Walk with me.'

She held out her hand, it was the most natural thing in the world for me to do and I reached out. Her hand felt cool yet welcoming. Over her shoulder she carried a raffia type bag, and as we walked I could hear the corn clicking together behind us as the field seemed to go on forever. At last, we stopped, and with a grace that belied her seeming age she took a blanket from her bag and spread it on the ground.

I listened as she talked about her life. Of how she fell in love and married her husband, the kind of life she'd had. Her children, and her grandchildren. All of whom she loved dearly. But most of all she talked about her childhood.

As I sat there she seemed to go all dreamy as she spoke of the things she would have liked to have done, travel and the like. The more she appeared absorbed in her thoughts the more distant she became. Then suddenly she stood up. 'We must go now!'

I was startled, but not unduly so. We rose and walked silently back to the stile, a silence like that of friends - needing no explanation.

As we reached the stile, she put her arm around my shoulders and gave me a gentle hug. Being a bit of a tomboy, this was something I would not normally tolerate, but coming from her I had no such qualms, being entirely comfortable with it.

'See you tomorrow,' she said.

I couldn't wait, and school was even more of a pain than usual, for some reason my English teachers never seemed to be on my wavelength, I was not alone, at least four other pupils had the same problem.

Anyway I was glad when the end of the school day came, it was late August and the evenings where long and warm, no such thing as homework I rushed my tea and did my chores before heading for the lane, hoping to be there before she came, I was early, but even so she was there.

'Hi, have you had a good day?' She looked at me her head cocked to one side, eyes smiling.

I pulled a face. 'Not's so's you'd notice.' I shrugged and fell in beside her as we walked into the field.

'Care to talk about it,' she posed the question casually as if completely aware of my feelings about the subject.

'Not really.'

At this point and under any other circumstances I would have been extremely embarrassed at the mere suggestion of discussing my problem, but not with her, she understood me like she was my own grandmother.

Neither of us mentioned it again that day. Grandmother! The thought hit me like a slap in the face. True, the way she seemed to appear and disappear was a bit weird and thoughts of ghosts and spirits had hung around in my mind though I refused to dwell on them. But no! She was far too real for that, we had a real relationship and a closeness I had never felt with anyone before.

I dismissed the thought from my mind - almost, a little niggle stayed there. Why didn't I find it scary? The way she seemed to fade away, after all she did remind me of my gran, although she was far too tall, neither did her clothes fit the picture in my mind. If she was a ghost, why was she here? What did she want?

The next day she was there as usual, same clothes, same spot, but with an air of sadness about her, the smile was missing. 'Hi, had a good day?' She looked over her shoulder.

'So, so, I've had better.' The greeting was almost ritual, and once over we walked into the cornfield.

'Be ready for harvest soon,' she said rubbing an ear of corn between her fingers.

I grabbed the bull by the horns. 'Who are you?' I blurted out, suddenly realising after all this time I didn't know her name.

She looked at me all wistful like. 'You wouldn't believe me if I told you.'

'Y-you are real?' I stammered feeling stupid.

'Real! What's real?' she shrugged, not the answer I expected, I thought for sure she would deny it hotly, this kind of passive acceptance took the wind out my sails.

'What's your name?' I must have sounded rude, because she looked at me with raised eyebrows.

'Valerie, the same as you,' she said.

'Oh! You remind me of my grandmother,' I said lamely.

'Do I?' This time mischievously.

I thought she was poking fun at me and started to sulk.

'You know you said you had a problem at school?' she glanced at me.

'Yes,' I felt myself going pink.

'Well that's something else we have in common, I have never been able to read or write but in my day they just put it down to laziness or lack of intelligence, it was nothing of the kind.

Only in later years have people come to realise that there is a scientific reason for it, like deafness or blindness it's a disability that affects personal communication and its technical name is dyslexia, an inability to stabilise letters to make words in a constant form.'

'Are you still dys . . . whatever it was you said it was?'

'Oh yes, I've learned to live with it, other senses seem to take over and I sometimes feel I'm blessed with a greater perception of things than most.'

She could have sounded pompous, but she didn't, she was very sincere and spoke simply and matter of factly.

We spoke a great deal about dyslexia, and I felt a great weight lift from my shoulders, I wasn't thick, or the dunce of the class, there was a valid reason for my lack of progress in school. In sheer relief I just cried and cried.

She just held me to her bosom until I was all dried up. I fell asleep against her breast and had no idea of the time when I awoke, except that it was dusk and she was rocking me gently back and forth. 'I have to go now, will you be OK?'

I sat up rubbing my eyes, 'Yes, I'm OK, anyway my mom will be wondering where I've got to.'

She looked at her watch and then at the cornfield glowing grey in the twilight. 'I have to go!' she stood up quickly. 'I really have to go now!' She lifted her hand and turned to go.

I'd watched her before without registering her going as strange. This time I concentrated as she moved through the corn, every other time seemed vague and uncertain, nothing I could identify. But this time she really did fade away into the corn, long before she should have gone out of sight. Then I was sure, she was a ghost. Afraid? No I was not, more like strangely comforted, like when a favourite aunt has been to visit, and sorted things out that your mother never got around to.

Saturday came and I walked up to the stile as usual, and there she was, leaning on the stile. 'Hi, had a good day?'

'Yeah, better now.' My enthusiasm must have shown because she had that wistful look in her eyes again.

'I'm glad, I must say you're looking better.' She put her arm round my shoulder and we walked to our customary spot.

She seemed more thoughtful than usual as she spread the blanket on the ground, we chatted away however about this and that, not once mentioning the evening before, or the strange way in which she came and went.

I did notice how she kept looking at her watch, and the way she held tight to a small cuddly toy. A rabbit stitched and patched with loving care. I didn't pay much attention to it as she had it mostly covered in her long fingered hands.

A skylark was singing high in the sky and a magpie flew chattering across in front of us low enough to sway the corn with its wings. I could hear a fire engine somewhere in the distance and an ambulance siren wailing away.

She stood up, 'I have to go,' she looked over her shoulder and smiled that smile, I knew I would never see her again as she walked into the corn.

The fire engine had been called to a house that burned down, my home, where I would normally have been home alone. It was when the fireman handed me my little rabbit, normally kept on my pillow that I knew who she really was . . .

Valerie was me fifty years from now!

A MAJOR CHANGE IN DIRECTION
Stephen J Bolton

Under normal circumstances Angelina was a very streetwise young woman, but at this moment in time she felt just like a fish out of water!

She didn't feel totally at home at the university students' reunion party. Everyone present had graduated from the same university around ten years ago and had individually followed entirely different careers!

Angelina couldn't help herself realising that nearly everyone present was trying to make the story of their success a little more than it was worth! It seemed that party A wouldn't be outdone by party B, or vice versa!

She was here for two reasons. Firstly a friend of hers whom she'd met at evening class had persuaded Angelina to go along to the party to give the guests some good entertainment with her excellent violin skills. Secondly she was here for her own reasons too! She hoped that an unattached career man would be present, in order for her to manipulate into her life. As the friend wasn't present Angelina knew that she could really let her hair down, without inhibition! She was now thirty one years old and beginning to desperately desire to change her life! With abilities only known to herself she would surely be able to change her suitor's life as well? Her ability could be used for either good or bad. She hoped that she would be able to keep things good and change both lives for the better! Instantly Angelina decided to keep her eyes and ears open for a respectable man who seemed to manage or own a developing business!

However the young lady wasn't anywhere near as respectable as she appeared to be portraying and if anything she was an expert with the flannel. This also applied to her appearance and Angelina had completely carried it off owing to the fact that she'd been afraid to get several tattoos done, when she was a teenager, unlike her wild female cronies. Also despite her days of aggressive fighting she fortunately hadn't lost nor damaged any teeth, neither had she been inflicted any permanent facial scars! One day she became lazy with her hair and let it grow from a skinhead crop into an elegant shoulder length style! For the first time in her life she found that she'd enough hair to learn to experiment with. Angelica also got used to skilfully applying cosmetics.

Gradually she fell in love with the feminine, cherubic image, which stared back at her from a mirror!

Once she realised her beauty potential Angelina ditched her tomboy glad rags and decided to try to become a cute little lady. With special effort she was sure that she could dissolve her past and here she was tonight, determined to put the icing on the cake. The only people, who knew that her real name was Agnes was her family and to cap it all Agnes seemed an old fashioned name, which she'd never really liked. As far as she was concerned Angelina sounded much more sophisticated. Especially in the company of select party guests like these!

Initially no one seemed to notice the cherubic like lady dressed in virgin white! It was a real pity, for Angelina had made a great effort with her appearance tonight. She was elegantly dressed in a white silk blouse, a short white cotton skirt that revealed her beautiful shapely legs, a white pair of high heeled shoes and she completed this outfit off with a matching white handbag. Her shoulder length hair was dangling loosely about her shoulders in a cascading mane of soft curls and if she said it herself, she looked a million dollars!

Therefore she decided that the time had come for her to introduce herself, regarding her violin performance, which she'd vowed to surprise the party guests with! Only Angelina herself knew that, when she was a youth learning to play the violin was the only civilised activity, which she'd allowed herself to indulge in behind closed doors! Slowly she took her perfectly tuned instrument from its wooden case, accompanied by the bow. She'd perfected many tunes and already had in mind, which she would start with.

Suddenly Angelina clapped her hands and asked the roomful of strangers if she could have their attention. After a short delay the room fell silent and all eyes were fixed upon her as she began to self introduce her proposed act! Already she felt a man's gaze and it was clear that he already found her fascinating! 'Good evening ladies and gentlemen,' she continued, 'I know we don't know each other yet, but I've been invited here tonight as a guest to provide you all with some live entertainment. It's my pleasure to entertain you all with my violin skills. I'd like to announce that I'm an experienced player and just like you folks I'm a graduate too! After my performance there's no doubt that you'll all be acquainted with the subject of my degree!' As she picked up her fiddle and bow with her dainty and well manicured hands, prior to her first chord already everyone gave her a round of applause. 'Right folks here's the first piece from Angelina,' she announced!

Already Marcus Sandiman felt himself rapidly falling under her spell. His fantasies and dreams were already beginning to take effect. How he was melted by the sight of this cute, little slimly-built lady with her head of elegant, long, shining curls. Of course, he realised that he shouldn't get carried away so soon, but he couldn't help feeling that she was his goal!

First of all Angelina performed Trios Gynopades, the First Movement, for the guests and everyone seemed to be very appreciative. Naturally, this inspired her to play several more classical pieces and a few country and western tunes. Everyone was fascinated regarding the speed which she could fluently play at. Angelina moved the bow back and forth across the strings almost quicker than the human eye could follow. Even an expert wouldn't have been able to have faulted her changes and rhythm! There wasn't a body in the room that wasn't impressed with her performance!

The more she played the more relaxed and inspired she became. During Angelina's performance Marcus edged his way to the front and tried his best to attract the cute little lady's attention. He managed that alright and during her final tune, the violinist gave him a heart-warming smile. Already he felt himself beginning to melt!

After Angelina had finished her performance the room burst into a prolonged round of applause! Before long everyone was gathering around her and offering to buy her a drink. People began to enthusiastically chat with her and she was already beginning to keep them entertained with her non-stop flannel!

Eventually Marcus managed to start chatting with Angelina and the first thing he did was to compliment her regarding her violin skills. After thanking Marcus and shaking hands with him, she introduced herself in more detail. She told him that she was a music graduate, who was a private violin tutor. She went on to explain that she wrote her own music, which wasn't totally a lie! Marcus already loved the feminine, delicate touch of her hand and hoped that he would get to hold it for longer in the near future.

Angelina listened enthusiastically as Marcus introduced himself to her. He explained that he was a self employed accountant who was working towards a chartered qualification in the profession. Above all, he was a divorcee whose wife had left him eighteen months ago. At the moment his only real joy was the fortnightly access, which he had to his two young daughters. Angelina immediately sensed that he was lonely and badly needing a woman's company, touch and possibly intimacy! As she chatted with Marcus the more satisfied she became that he was showing her promise! Especially with his profession and business managing skills! As they chatted Angelina looked Marcus up and down and had to be honest with herself that the tall, blond and blue-eyed man was fairly attractive and sophisticated in her eyes! Already she strongly sensed that she could well have found what she was looking for. When she falsely told him about her life, Angelina was rather fuelled with mischievous thoughts. Especially as there seemed to be no doubt that he'd already taken her at face value! Initially she felt a bit of a fraud. She didn't quite understand though that Marcus was a bit of a dreamer towards the type of lady, which she was trying to portray! Instantly though, she reminded herself of tonight's mission, which of course was her main concern. Now that the door seemed to be slightly ajar, her natural instinct was to try and open it much further!

The majority of the guests soon respected that their guest violinist had found a new friend and that she would wish to spend some time with him. Eventually both parties were left to enjoy each others company. The couple already sensed that they would like to sleep together and discover each other. However, the time for that hadn't come yet! Before long something else began to take place, now that the initial buffet and violin performance were both over. As he'd already promised one of the guests he'd brought along his DJ equipment and CD collection.

'Ladies and gentlemen,' he announced, 'now for the second part of tonight's entertainment. I'll be playing for all of you, music of your choice till the death! If anyone's got any requests I'll be delighted to play them.' After his initial announcement the hall was filled with an old 1970s classic, *Rock Your Baby* by George McRae. As far as the DJ was concerned that record would be a brilliant ice-breaker. He proved himself to be right too, for one by one people shuffled towards the dance floor and began to cavort in front of the pulsating, coloured lights.

Marcus respected that it was always customary for the man to ask the lady for the first dance and naturally this was what he asked Angelina. 'Sure, lead the way,' she smiled. Marcus felt he was walking on air for he hadn't done this since he was twenty-one! The couple began their dance and it was obvious within the first few seconds that Angelina had the better skills in this field. If anything, he was moving mechanically and well out of time. Angelina chose to ignore this and to carry on! They danced their way through several more records and then before they knew where they were, it was time for the final smooches! Marcus debated in his mind whether he should ask her for a close dance or not. However, he ended up asking her anyway, Angelina smiled and just whispered, 'Okay.'

The couple held each other and began to slowly move around the dance floor to the old Bee Gees classic *How Deep Is Your Love?* Once again Angelina realised that she shouldn't really be here in the arms of this man. However, she reminded herself once again that if she wanted to change her life, then this would just have to be! As far as Marcus was concerned he was simply delighted that such a sweet, attractive, little lady had supposedly taken such a shine to him. He hadn't yet asked Angelina about her private life, but he felt quite sure that she was unattached! Owing to the fact he'd already consumed several beers, he already felt bold enough to cuddle her really close and to stroke her long, curly hair. *It's now or never,* thought Angelina as she initiated a long, lingering, teenager-fashioned kiss with Marcus. Immediately she could almost read his thoughts. She knew that all she had to do was to get a little closer to him and she would be able to find out more about him. It would probably be to her advantage!

Meanwhile, the party guests couldn't help but respect how things seemed to have quickly developed between the couple. Many women thought, *ah how cute, love at first sight!* When the dancing came to an end both parties were really glad that they were with somebody. Soon they were exchanging mobile phone numbers. They both checked that their newly entered digits made the opposite phone ring. Angelina then collected her precious violin and her coat.

'May we share a taxi home Angelina?' asked Marcus shyly.

'Not tonight,' she replied, 'I never allow men whom I've only just met to have too much leeway on our first meeting. Sorry, but it's just the way I was brought up!' In all fairness she thought that this man did deserve some respect. After all, he wasn't a bit like all the other lowlifes that she'd spent her time with. No, this one had to be handled in the right way, at least until she'd found out enough about him anyway!

'Okay then Angelina, I'll call you tomorrow night and then hopefully we can arrange a future meeting and get to know each other better,' suggested Marcus.

'Well for now, thanks for the memory,' replied Angelina. 'However, a text message would be great,' she hinted.

When all was said and done they'd already booked separate taxis beforehand! They both settled for a goodnight kiss and Marcus gave Angelina a repeat compliment about her violin playing. As things turned out Angelina's taxi arrived first, so Marcus was able to see her off. She was rather taken aback as he kissed her on the cheek, opened the cab door for her and slipped her ten pounds towards her taxi fare. 'Oh you shouldn't have,' she exclaimed! Then she added, 'Don't forget my text message though!' Presently the black and white vehicle drove off into the night with Angelina waving to her newly found friend. At least she supposed that, that's what she could call Marcus!

An hour later Marcus arrived back at his cold, empty flat. He didn't notice the pin-drop silence for he was in an alcohol induced haze. He went into his bedroom on automatic pilot. Already he was keying out his text message, which he hoped Angelina was still waiting for. He was hoping that tonight's meeting would possibly be a change in his life's direction. Since his divorce he hadn't had much luck in the relationships field. This was mainly because most of his weekends were taken up by entertaining his two children. How lovely it was to be able to just think of himself for once. Marcus texted the final word and pressed send. As the word 'sent' appeared on his phone console, he smiled and wished himself luck!

Angelina was just getting into her frumpy pyjamas, when her mobile phone bleeped. She pressed open and smiled as the awaited text message showed.

Hi Angelina, hope U arrived home OK. Gud nite, sleep well, nice 2 have met U, will think of U 2nite & call U 2moz.

'Aw how sweet,' laughed Angelina to herself. 'Though we mustn't leave it too long before we next meet. I think I'll get to like you Marcus, but I'll need you for more than your body, I'm afraid! First though I'll need to glean some more information from you about your life. Then sooner or later I'll drop the bombshell!'

Poor Marcus, he simply had no idea that Angelina had a mysterious psychic gift. All she needed to do was to sleep with someone and get close to them in order to glean their darkest secrets from them. Unfortunately, she also knew many undesirable people and vile blackmail plots were not entirely out of the question! Also Marcus had no notion that the cute, little cherub, which Angelina loved to pose as, was simply a mask of bluff to the world. He'd already become smitten and to make matters worse, she was already in his dreams tonight.

Angelina looked around at her violin and viola collection, which included an electric instrument with an amplifier. She was actually a member of a band line up and like anybody with ambition they were hoping to break into the big time. What both she and the band needed was someone to manage their finances and to be able to negotiate deals for them. The band already had some contact with the music industry, but a person who was highly experienced with organising finances was vital! As soon as Angelina had discovered Marcus' occupation, it wasn't any surprise that she wouldn't let him go!

When she'd kissed Marcus on the dance floor a vision had already entered her mind. Unfortunately at the beginning of his career he'd got into a major business disagreement with two men who initially unknown to him were rogues! After they'd made several vile threats to Marcus, he was forced to flee the area and to begin again somewhere new. Unknown to him both these two sinister men still held a grudge against him! If ever they caught up with him their horrible revenge plot would still be in existence! Angelina hadn't yet grasped the full details. However, once she'd slept with Marcus all would be revealed to herself. Sooner or later with the help of other undesirables, she would be able to deliver to him a blackmail bribe!

If everything went to plan both parties would undergo a major change in direction, this thought was in Angelina's mind as she snuggled down into bed. As she drifted into slumber she thought about how she would hopefully soon seduce Marcus in this very room!

Meanwhile, Marcus was too alone with his thoughts and it was true that he deeply desired Angelina, how he adored cute, little cherubic women with long hair! However, he also recognised the fact that Angelina had professional musician potential! No doubt she had lingering ambitions about hitting the big time, after all she had both the skills, personality and the looks! Marcus was content with being an accountant, but in his life he needed more excitement and he felt that if someone was willing to give him a chance he could become a good manager in the music business.

After all, he'd fleeced two big guys once and he realised that if he got the chance to become a big time band manager he could do it again, big style. Yes, Angelina was a cunning little con woman, but it was the first time in her life that she'd ever met anyone like Marcus. Maybe Angelina wasn't the only party in this potential relationship, who was thinking of a major change in direction!

UNDERPASS
Guy Fletcher

I am alone in the house now, listening to sombre music. My wife is in work and my dear child happily ensconced in the nursery, a million moons away from fear and shame.

I remember climbing up Snowdonia on a glorious summer's day some years back and the breathtaking view carried for many a mile, in those days my life seemed to be as clear and beautiful. But then dark clouds suddenly drifted in a menacing fashion, first of all causing the mountains to be painted with a dark shadow and then enveloping the once azure sky and now my view became restricted to a few metres. The point, of course, is that when life is at its most settled and wonderful, the fall is so much greater and one careless step and I could have plunged from the clouds on that grand mountain. Life can be like a rose soaking up the summer sun and then plucked by a schoolboy's grubby hands.

In fact, my existence only careered into freefall the day before yesterday. This was a day which started well enough, I was in an ebullient mood after gaining promotion.

'Don't drink too much tonight, I know what you're like,' my wife Sarah had said as I left for work in the morning.

'I'll try not to get off with any schicksas,' I jokingly retorted.

That morning I left the car at home and caught the bus. I had an uncomfortable journey standing in the aisle and when the bus braked sharply due to an errant motorist, I landed embarrassingly in the lap of a young woman.

'I'm really sorry.'

'Don't be, I rather enjoyed it.'

She and her friend then laughed, making me feel even more of a prat. I noticed all of the lone motorists clogging up the roads and felt a slight pang of guilt for I was usually one of them. I didn't realise then that my guilt would be magnified a thousand times or more. I arrived at work five minutes late much to the delight of the lugubrious Adam.

'Not much of an impression for the boss's pet,' he sneered.

'Oh beware, my lord of jealousy; it is the green-eyed monster which doth mock the meat it feeds on.'

'You what!' He then muttered something under his bitter breath which I chose to ignore. It would take more than an embittered work colleague and a late bus to put me off my stride. The day soon ended and at 6 o'clock I was enjoying a delicious ice-cold Grolsch in the local. 'Adam not coming then?' asked Johnny our resident stirrer, knowing full well he wasn't coming.

'He said he had better things to do,' I replied.

'Miserable b*****d,' said Carla, already on her second double vodka I noticed.

'Yes, he does make Scrooge seem like the laughing policeman,' I pointed out.

The hours flew by and suddenly I was left with just Carla who I promised my colleagues I would call a taxi for.

'I've split up with Paul,' she said, crying into her vodka.

'It didn't take an Einstein to work that one out. I'm sorry.'

'Don't be, actually I'm glad we're alone. I've always fancied you. Come to my flat, you won't regret it.'

I was tempted, believe me. I'm a happily married man and yet I almost took her up on the offer. Carla is a beautiful girl but then I thought of my wife and child.

'Ah, but I would regret it though, I'll get you a taxi.'

After Carla stumbled in an unladylike manner into the taxi, I felt rather smug. Here was I, newly promoted, a stunning wife and kid and furthermore a beautiful girl with a crush on me whom I'd 'nobly' fended off, what a man! Now I feel I detest the man of that moment almost as much as the one later on. The evening was cold and an unpleasant rain attempted unsuccessfully to sober me up. I swayed down the street singing happily to myself, a man on top of the world. I was not in the least concerned as I approached the uninviting underpass with its indecipherable graffiti and perennial reek of urine.

'Let me go, please,' came a desperate voice.

'Oh we will, but not just yet,' said a malevolent youth.

I noticed there were three hooded youths and a short-skirted blonde girl. A piercing screech emitted from their victim, a young Asian lad. Now I was sober, stone-cold sober and my heart was beating like drums played by a man on speed.

'Just leave him alone,' I said weakly.

'Walk on by Mr Suit or you'll get the same treatment. You want some eh?' the ringleader snarled. He had cold blue eyes and a scar running down the left side of his face. Although I was bigger he looked well versed in the art of street fighting, which I was not.

'Please mister, help me.' I looked into the lad's eyes, but just walked on by and bizarrely the song of that name played in my head. I heard the girl laugh and also a derogatory term involving sex alone. I was tempted to go back but my morals had deserted me now, unlike earlier in the evening.

'Why should I get involved?' I said to myself. 'Then both of us would have been beaten up.' When I was a little way from the scene I reached for my mobile but the battery was flat, so I ran towards a phone box. I raced across the road without looking, causing a car to brake suddenly and again an expletive flew my way. Typically the phone was not working and it was only ten minutes later that I managed to call the police. The last bus had long since gone, so I took a taxi home.

'Had a good night Sir?'

'Eventful,' I replied quietly.

My wife was still up watching the late night movie. I let my unpleasant experience fade from my memory like condensation on a window and put my arms around my wife, a picture of suburban bliss and light years away from the underpass.

That night a nightmare invaded my sleep. I was walking under the underpass on a bright, sunny day when I was surrounded by the gang I had the misfortune to encounter earlier.

'It's your turn now, Mr Hero,' said the scarred youth menacingly.

Yes, I am alone in the house now listening to sombre music. In front of me is a newspaper. The headline attracts me like flies to manure. *Asian youth found dead in undergrowth.* They showed a picture of a smiling, shy-looking youth who was now lying bloodied and battered in the morgue. If I had aided him he would probably still be alive and the thought made me gulp with shame.

Apparently he had hit his head whilst falling after a vicious attack. The culprits were still at large and I know that I could identify the youth with the scar and probably the girl too. Yes, it was time to do my 'duty' and be shown up as a coward, the only chance that poor lad had. I drove towards the police station a far less smug man.

LIGHTING OUT
Terence Leslie

George was up in the lamproom of the Whiterock lighthouse which stood on an island at the mouth of the Bristol Channel.

It was evening and the sun was dipping into the Atlantic far to the west like a slice of orange in a cocktail. Suddenly, he heard the whirring sound of a helicopter. Scratching his head he muttered, 'Strange, the relief ain't due for another week.'

He completed his task of checking over the lenses, prisms and mechanisms then rushed down the winding steps to the living quarters. There he found his colleagues, Harry and Albert, sitting at a table.

'Here, you two hear that helicopter fly past a few minutes ago?' he asked.

'Yes, we heard it. Thought it was the coastguard or the boys from Culrose out on exercise.'

'Think I'd better take a look outside just in case,' George answered.

'But dinner's ready,' Albert chimed in. 'Can't you wait till we've eaten?'

'You keep the dinner warm. I'll be back in a jiffy,' George added.

'I'll come as well,' said Harry, 'just in case there's something fishy going on.'

George went outside. As Harry reached over a chair to retrieve his pipe from the table a shot rang out. Unnerved by the sound he knocked the chair sideways. 'Bloody hell, what's going on?' he shouted.

Albert crept over to the door and cautiously peered outside. An alarming scene met his gaze. George was standing stock-still halfway to the heliport. A helicopter had landed and two armed men were standing over a prostrate figure. The lighthouse man was just deciding whether to make a dash for cover when one of the gunmen spotted him. Raising his gun the man shouted, 'Stay where you are or you'll get the same.' George remained motionless. The gunman continued, 'OK, we're coming over. Don't move.'

His accomplice picked the prostrate figure in a fireman's lift. As the two approached George could see that the figure being carried wore a Securicor uniform. *Must have been a hold-up*, he thought.

Then to the gunmen he shouted, 'Look fellas, whatever you're doing here is none of my business. Why don't you and your mate just leave?'

'We're going to hole up here for a couple of days, so shut your mouth,' said the gunman. Then to his mate, 'Let's get him into the lighthouse out of sight.'

'You! Move!' he snapped at George and threatened him with the gun. The group moved slowly towards the lighthouse.

Two figures emerged from behind the helicopter, each armed with a large piece of rock. Stealthily they crept up behind the gunmen. Two arms swung and two heads caved in.

'Show's over George,' Harry said.

'Where the hell did you spring from?' George gasped as he spun round.

'Albert told me what was going on so we sneaked out of the lighthouse and crept round behind you under the shelter of the rocks. Saved yer bacon didn't we?' Harry added with big grin on his face.

'Better check out the chopper to make sure there's no more bodies inside,' Albert said.

They walked back to the helicopter and Albert climbed inside. A few minutes later he re-emerged with a shocked look on his face. 'Guess what I've found?' he shouted down.

'What?' George called back.

'Sacks of money. Tens, twenties and fifties. Must be nearly half a million quid here. What are we going to do with it?'

Harry smirked, 'Know anything about helicopters Albert?'

'Sure do. Did my bit in the Falklands flying Sea Kings. You two know anything about money?'

'Know how to spend it,' George replied.

'Right then,' said Harry, 'let's go visit Sydney and Alice.'

'Who are they?' Albert asked, 'relatives of yours?'

'No dope. They're in Australia.'

'Better still,' George interrupted, 'let's do a Ronnie Biggs and light out for Rio de Janeiro.'

A few days later a Trinity House helicopter landed on Whiterock to investigate the un-manned lighthouse. The crew did not notice a rat gnawing at a rope. The strands parted and three body-filled bags sank slowly into the sea.

THE STORM
Aaron Tomes (11)

It's 2004, but let's go back three years. Edward Carnaby is going to visit his grandparents on Shadow Island. Edward doesn't know that the day he goes is the day of the storm. Edward is a single guy who lives in Los Angeles and he is a car racer.

The day before the visit, 8pm.
The phone rang. 'Edward, are you there?' said a voice.
'Yeah, I'm here,' answered Edward.
'Are you racing tonight?' asked his friend Stevo.
'No, I have to sort things out for tomorrow,' replied Edward.
'Why?' shouted Stevo sounding disappointed. 'You said you would race today.'
'Sorry Stevo,' said Edward, 'I'm going on holiday to where my grandparents live.'
'Okay,' said Stevo. 'I understand. See you in a week mate, bye.'

The Airport
Edward is at the airport waiting for the plane which would take him to Shadow Island. 'Your attention please,' boomed a voice overhead. 'All passengers for Shadow Island boarding in ten minutes.'

Edward felt a little nervous about the flight and the dark clouds gathering on the horizon didn't make him feel any better. As he boarded the plane the first fat raindrops began to fall and a gust of wind blew sharply. He felt sure that there was more to come. As the wind blew stronger, the little plane was buffeted across the sky. The pilot tried to reassure the passengers, but Edward heard the note of panic in his voice.

Edward looked out of his window and saw big, black clouds and streaks of lightning. He was scared. He knew they were going to crash. There was a rumble, then a jerk. The plane fell towards the sea, spiralling round and round. A passenger opened the door and jumped out and the rest of the passengers began to follow. Edward was the last to jump and as he fell through the darkness he felt sure that this was the end.

As Edward began to pass out he thought he was hallucinating when he felt arms around his waist and the sensation of drifting rather than falling. He thought maybe he was dead and this was Heaven. Then he felt a cold splash of water and he realised he was in the sea . . . *alone.* He turned to see who had saved him, but there was nobody there.

Edward saw a bright light on the shore and swam towards it. As he was helped out of the water he realised it was his grandfather as he finally fainted with exhaustion.

Edward woke with a start in a warm, cosy bed with his grandfather by his side. 'I don't know how you survived Edward?' said his grandfather. 'It's a miracle.'

'This is going to sound crazy,' said Edward, 'but I felt arms around me as I fell and a voice said it's going to be okay.'

His grandfather turned very pale. 'During the war,' he said, 'a man called Jack saved my life during a parachute jump when my chute didn't open properly. As I fell he held me round the waist and said those very same words. The funny thing is I heard from a friend today that Jack died of old age last night. I wonder . . . '

WHAT GOES AROUND, COMES AROUND
Mick Nash

Lennie was built like a bean pole. He hefted his big kit bag on his shoulder with obvious effort and strain. His pal, Pete, much more stockily built, wore a rucksack, which was much easier to manage and far more comfortable as they trudged along the road leading up the wooded hillside. Pete's head turned at the sound of an approaching car. He stuck out his thumb in the hope of a lift. The car slowed and stopped beside the two lads, who both sighed a prayer of thanks, especially Lennie. Pete opened the rear door and they clambered in gratefully and shut the door and settled down. The car, a big estate car loaded with what seemed to be fishing gear, moved off. The man in the front passenger seat turned and looked at the boys in the back. 'Hey Hal, look at those kids!' The driver looked round and gasped in amazement. As he did so, the car veered off the road and went down a steep embankment out of control. When the car hit a tree and stopped, Pete opened his door, grabbed Lennie's arm and pulled him clear. There was a whooshing sound as the car caught light, then a loud *bang* as it exploded in flames.

Lennie pulled out his cell-phone and hit 999 asking for all three services urgently. The police and fire engine arrived quickly with an ambulance not far behind. The police spoke to the two boys, while the firemen extinguished the car and sent the ambulance away as the two men in the car were well past needing it. Lennie and Pete gave their statements to the police and thanked whatever deity protects hitch-hiking campers. The mood for their camping jaunt was gone, so they accepted a lift home in the police car.

The two boys, close friends since primary school, stayed close mates through school and college, and went into business together many years later, running a record company with an occasional hit record boosting their profits.

Eventually, they both got married and raised families. Their close friendship did not diminish and they regularly went fishing together, which they found relaxing and pleasant, although the fish probably didn't see it that way, being hoisted out of their environment with a hook stuck through their faces.

After a particularly good financial year, Lennie and Pete decided to have a fishing holiday together, trout fishing in the hilly area where their youthful tragedy had occurred and where they had not been since.

They loaded up Pete's big Toyota estate car and bade farewell to their families before setting off. Halfway up a long hill as they neared their destination, they saw a couple of kids thumbing a ride and Pete slowed and stopped to pick them up. The two lads clambered in the back. As Pete pulled away, Lennie noticed that the two lads in the back were spitting images of himself and Pete when they had hitched a lift all those years before. 'Hey Pete, look at those kids!'

Pete looked round and gasped in amazement. As he did so, the car veered off the road and went down a steep embankment out of control. When the car hit a tree and stopped, one of the kids opened his door and dragged his mate out of the car just before it burst into flames and exploded . . .

THE PASSENGER ON FLIGHT F414
Elizabeth Boultwood

The Christmas carols were interrupted: 'Will all passengers for the II-30 flight, F414 to Prestwick please proceed to the waiting lounge at Gate 33. Thank you.' The nasal tones rang out over the tannoy.

Daphne had arrived at Stansted with only minutes to spare, the traffic on the way in had been very heavy; then there had been her bag search and herself being frisked, when the gold-coloured necklace she'd been wearing set off the alarm as she'd entered the main part of the airport. The woman on duty there had been steely-eyed and cold when she spoke to Daphne telling her to 'spread your arms', in comparison, the woman handling the bag search was warm and chatty asking, 'Are you going to Scotland for business or for pleasure?'

'It's pleasure,' Daphne had replied.

Well, here she was at last, sitting with her coffee waiting to board the aircraft. She looked at her fellow travellers warily, thinking as she always did before flying, *are these my companions into the next world?* And she shivered at the thought.

She noticed that there were several small children and babies with their parents, a nun, a group of young men with cans of lager and a young couple, obviously newly-weds with eyes only for each other. The rest of the passengers were assorted couples and she also noticed in a far corner, an elderly lady holding a huge bunch of roses. She appeared to be sleeping as her head was drooping into the flowers.

A nasal command was aired once more and people arose and made their way through the doors that led to the corridors leading towards the waiting aircraft. Daphne flourished her boarding slip and thronged with the rest. She had only an overnight bag which held her party wear. Her allocated seat number was 21.

After alighting the steps and entering the plane she was greeted by a stewardess in a warm and welcoming manner. Seat 21 was reached, it was the aisle seat on a row of three. The window seat, number 19, was occupied by . . . a single red rose!

Putting away her bag and coat in the overhead cupboard, Daphne made herself comfortable. She let her mind drift to her destination. Her brother was celebrating fifty years of marriage. A golden wedding.

They hadn't seen each other for twenty years! Safety belts on, the plane took to the air. Daphne was always relieved when they were actually in the air.

Whoops! A little turbulence buffeted the aircraft and she opened her eyes. Gosh. She must have dozed off. Good Lord! There was someone sitting in seat 19! It was a small, old lady with white hair arranged in a bun at the back of her head. She was wearing gold-wired spectacles and had a Blackwatch tartan shawl around her shoulders. In her left arm, nearest Daphne, was a bunch of red roses with a very powerful scent. She appeared to be sleeping. It was the old lady she had noticed in the lounge. *But how did she get there without waking me up?* Daphne wondered. She shivered and pulled her jacket across her chest and fastened her buttons . . . it had suddenly got colder. She closed her eyes again. It seemed like only a moment when she was awakened by the captain's voice telling the passengers to fasten their seat belts as they were approaching Prestwick. Their one hour journey was ending. Dutifully she did this and glancing to her right to see if the old lady was suitably belted she was amazed to find only the single rose on the seat! The woman had done it again . . . she'd moved without disturbing her.

The stewardess was checking on the passengers and Daphne told her, 'The lady occupying seat 19 hasn't come back yet.'

The stewardess looked at her with an odd expression on her face and said, 'But the two seats next to you have been empty throughout the entire flight.'

Daphne was astonished and began to describe the missing passenger. The stewardess paled and told Daphne that she would have a word with her when the aircraft landed.

It transpired that, three Christmas's ago, there had been a passenger fitting the description, on her way to visit her grandchildren, but she had passed away with heart failure during the flight, in seat 19 on this aircraft. Today, was the anniversary of her death. Although shocked, Daphne was also thrilled to discover that she'd seen a *ghost.* This was something to tell her grandchildren.

The stewardess offered her a brandy and she accepted gratefully, definitely stirred and visibly shaken when the red rose began to fade away before her eyes.

HOMEWARD BOUND
J W Whiteacre

Last train, last chance. Mixed bag of bodies push and more push. Lots of chatter. Those returning from the theatre, bars, loved ones. Pretending he is late from the office and thinking up excuses for his wife, the smooth, well-appointed seeks solace at the bar - his last hope saloon. Think bubbles leap from his tailored haircut. He's only four hours late for his dinner. His wife really doesn't understand him - not like the barmaid in his city club. He really must have another double gin - the usual routine of the first class pathetic.

The train is late leaving. They have problems loading parcels. This is the true part of the well-appointed's call but would you believe it, whilst holding a casserole for four long hours? You might think it one excuse too many.

The train gains speed and you wear the bruises of being thrown from side to side. Forced to listen to the prattle of the over-opinionated, those who insist you will hear. Forced to listen to the latest mobile ringing tones of those who need you to know they have an important call. Then you hear a quick burst of mobile Mozart and listen to the well-appointed making drunken sounds of love as he answers the barmaid's passion. Tell yourself *now* how well you can do without London, without the falsehood, without the people in love with themselves and their own voices. Tell yourself to return to the wilderness. It is time!

This is your final journey. Walking slowly to the bar, you remember the purpose of your travel; you recall just why you are on this train. Thinking how good dinner will be, however late the serving - the smooth, well-appointed, still blubbering into his mobile - receives his casserole. It mingles, drips, mingles with his well-tailored haircut and drops into his sixth double gin and tonic.

You sigh, you smile, you take a snap for the barmaid. *You* have just earned your exit, your BR Freedom ticket to roam. Nearby drunks rapidly move away as he splutters and groans - not in a very smooth, well-appointed way - you ponder - whether you went too far with that extra net of garlic bulbs - the two pots of pepper - the orange coloured tandoori mix - and your wedding ring he has just swallowed.

Pudding anyone?

ONWARD JOURNEY
Janice Melmoth

The clock chimed the hour as the train left the station and gathered momentum, swallowing the countryside like a hungry panther, intent only on following its prey. The pulsating sound coming from the great wheels embraced the occupants of the carriage as they settled down to enjoy their journey. One very tall gentleman dressed in a blue striped suit became rapidly engrossed in a collection of papers retrieved from a bulging, black briefcase. I noticed a mobile phone and deliberated the outcome if it were to ring!

In contrast, sitting next to him was a petite, grey-haired, elderly lady clutching a beige handbag twisting and turning the short strap, clearly anxious about a forthcoming meeting or perhaps an interview. She was dressed very formally in a pale blue suit with a matching floral blouse, I hoped the skirt was crease resistant.

Directly opposite sat a young couple oblivious to their surroundings, interested only in each other. He had a protective arm around her shoulder and his eyes shone with happiness, the ever popular jeans and baggy jumpers adorned their young bodies. Daylight was not being kind to the carriage for although the hour was early, we were devoid of sunlight. I hoped no one would want the light on . . .

The train stopped at three stations and the passengers remained seated, maybe they were all going to the end of the line. No one entered our carriage.

A sudden movement caused a flicker of interest as the city gent scooped up his papers and carefully replaced them in the briefcase before settling down once more and closing his eyes. This clearly disturbed the elderly lady who began to rummage in her handbag and eventually produced a squashed up sandwich wrapped in clingfilm.

The young couple shared a can of Coke which they managed without altering their position!

The comfortable silence had sent the elderly lady asleep still clutching her bag, whilst the city gent was snoring quietly with his arms firmly crossed, the young couple remained in their original position as the train chugged along the iron track, mile after mile after mile . . . What little daylight we started with was now not fading fast and the carriage was becoming quite cold. I started to wonder how long it would be before the occupants woke up as the cold air surrounded them?

The rolling landscape constantly changed colour with the hills looming high, yet seemingly near enough to touch, occasionally a building would rise up and the scenery would be interrupted with their dominant presence . . .

The passengers stirred and shivered as one-by-one they woke from their slumber, the journey continued with everyone fighting to stay awake.

Breaking the silence, the loud speaker boomed a deep, masculine voice announcing the pending arrival of the final station. No one seemed particularly anxious to escape the confines of the carriage and diligently sat and waited for the train to finish its expedition.

The great machine eventually ground to a half, thankful for a rest after its long journey . . . the surge of movement as passengers alighted from other carriages made little impact on the young couple as they sat engrossed and only intent on each other, the city gent and elderly lady remained seated.

Time seemed to stand still and yet in reality only a few minutes had passed before the final passengers emerged onto the platform and followed the dusty exit signs.

The carriage groaned with a sigh of relief as one-by-one limbs were stretched and bags were collected, discarded rubbish was sticking out between the seats and various packets and wrappings lay in untidy piles on the floor . . .

Ouch, that was a bumpy landing, I wish he would slow down, I am feeling quite queasy. He might be in a hurry, but there is no need to take it out on me, this crowd's getting bigger and faster, whoops, that's torn it, he's not going to be happy . . .

The day was rapidly coming to an end, and the evening sun was vanishing, swallowed by the horizon who wanted it for tomorrow. Everywhere people were hurrying with a sense of determination and importance. The gradual crescendo of laughter, coupled with the urgency of people with a purpose, an aim, or a goal. Maybe they had buses to catch or partners to meet, trains or planes, or just the solitude of an empty flat . . . most of them would return tomorrow to begin another day of jostling for space on the great iron machine that would once again tour through the countryside.

I used to have a purpose, I used to be needed, I used to have somewhere to go, somewhere to rest, but not now. The hustle and bustle belong to others, I can only watch and listen. After my bumpy landing I gained a vantage point. I could now watch people as they scurry past and glance over in my direction, often with a disdainful frown. Whether pitifully or scornfully I will never know, they are there for only a fleeting second before continuing their journey, somebody is waiting for them.

It's quite chilly now that the sun has disappeared and night-time has started to encapsulate what I begin to consider my domain . . . this is my third day and each one is pretty much the same, except that I am gathering people's unwanted debris around me. Depending on which way the wind is blowing determines how cold I get. Some days are better than others, some days I long for rain just to damp down the dust. The worst kind of weather is the cold north wind. He goes straight through me, I have no protection, and he has no conscience.

The silence descends once more, with an eerie void that hangs in the air waiting to tumble and cause havoc. I absorb this time like a thirsty sponge, time is of an essence. I really do not know how much longer I will be here, alone and unloved, with no purpose, no security and no future.

I look ahead with a vacant expression and realise that I have to change my pessimistic attitude and think positively, looking forwards and not looking back . . . what is around me? What has changed in the last few days? I am worth more than the dust that is settling around me. More than the wind that chills me to the core. I want and need love, I have so much love to give in return - why do people look at me with so much distaste and so much scorn?

Staring straight ahead I see a tall lady in a green coat, she is looking up at the clock, then nervously pacing up an down, yet keeping to a designated area. My interest was mounting by the minute, and I felt the ability to visualise her anxiety levels which must be rapidly rising as she alternately paced her chosen area and looked up at the clock . . .

I could feel my own apprehension rising and hoped that no one came along and blocked my view. Telling myself to remain calm and collective I settle down to await the 'meeting'. Ten minutes have now passed since my first sighting of the lady in the green coat . . . how long will she wait? How long can she wait?

In the distance is a figure hurrying towards the clock. I think it's a man, but I can't be certain. Yes it is, he's clutching something close to his chest, oh that's disconcerting, it's a hat . . . not very exciting!

The lady in green has witnessed his approach and turns . . . such a tender moment, they are clearly pleased to see each other. They embrace and try to have a conversation all at the same time! The man disengages himself and holds the lady at arm's length, he evidently has something of great importance to share with her. Leading her to a nearby wooden bench, he gently touches her cheek and eye contact is maintained. A rapid exchange of words takes place and their body language does not indicate what they are discussing. I become absorbed in their meeting and do not feel that I am intruding. I wish I was a little nearer, although had I been I would not have been the little girl approach. She was not very old, perhaps six or seven with long, blonde hair and striding purposely towards the bench she taps the man on his shoulder.

A lively conversation takes place before the little girl smiles and winds her arms around the man's neck. He hugs her tightly and looks up at the lady in green. A false smile begins to form on the lady's face and with a quick shrug of her shoulders she sits down. My apprehension and curiosity are mounting . . .

Wow! Has somebody turned the lights out? I turn from left to right, but still see nothing, except a suitcase! Oh my, of all the space a black blob has occupied mine! Resentment mounts as I am unable to move this great object and patience is not my best virtue.

Hours and hours go by, well it seems like that when you are waiting. In reality it was probably minutes before the black blob moved. The couple were holding hands, but where was the little girl? She wasn't with them, I began searching the crowds, surely she hasn't wandered off? I think my eyes are deceiving me, she appears to be coming this way . . . surely she can't have seen me. I am part of the fixtures covered in dust, cobwebs and things one does not like to think about!

Ouch! She has a good grip, any harder and my eyes will pop out.

'Daddy, Daddy, look what I've found.'

I get waved around and think a headache has my name on it!

'I can keep it can't I? Say yes Daddy, say yes . . . I can wash him and sew his eye back . . . please Daddy?'

The lady in green has remained silent, but reaches out to take me from the little girl, heavens, my life in her hands . . .

'He certainly needs a good wash, what do you think John? A lucky day all round.'

I could hardly breathe waiting for an answer. Someone wanted me, all eyes were focused on John, what was he going to say?

'Well, he certainly needs a wash, but I think I would prefer to buy a new one Tammy, he is so scruffy, leave him where you found him and we will go to the toy shop.'

'But Daddy, I don't want a new one, I want this one, *please* Daddy.'

The lady in the green coat whispers to John quietly, I thought it was rude to whisper, well maybe not in this case. 'Tammy, Daddy said you can keep it, providing it is thoroughly clean before you play with it . . . now put it in this bag and I will wash him and sew his eye back. You could name him Lucky if you want, after all it is a special day for everyone.'

Wow, it really is a lucky day, a new home and a new family. I'm sure Tammy can hear me purring . . .

FAMILY FEUD
Marcellina Boyle

'Mum that's the one.'

'Which?'

'The purple one, Family Feud.'

Oliver's mum, Mary, picks up the video game and takes a closer look. She turns it over and quickly scans the back cover.

'I don't know. It's got a parental guidance sticker.'

'It's okay Mum. Everyone in school's playing it.'

'That doesn't make it right.'

'Mum it's just a game . . . Please.'

'Okay, okay. I said I'd make up for your birthday party and I mean it this time.'

'So this is what you've been bangin' on about?' Oliver's dad, Bill, appears from nowhere and grabs the game from his wife's hand. He flicks it over dismissively and then shoves it at Oliver. 'Well come on then, let's pay for it and go. I should be playing golf.'

They all make their way through the quiet games shop to the tall thin man dressed in black T-shirt and faded jeans, standing behind the counter. Oliver hands him Family Feud as his dad pulls out his credit card. The man's eyebrows rise slightly on seeing the game.

'You do know this comes with a warning,' he says, with his eyes fixed down on Oliver.

'Yes, yes! Do you want our custom or not?' Oliver's dad replies impatiently.

Unfazed, the man's eyes remain on Oliver, who shifts uncomfortably on his feet. 'Just as long as you know . . . that will be £39.95.'

Oliver bursts into his bedroom, runs over to his TV, switches it on, dumps his bag at his feet, throws his coat on the floor, flops to his knees and hurriedly pulls Family Feud from his bag. He quickly loads it into his game console and sits back as it begins. The title sequence had barely started when his mother walks in.

'You didn't waste any time.'

Oliver doesn't respond.

'Your dad's gone to golf, and I'm off to meet the girls in the gym. I think your gran is on her way, so you won't be alone for long.'

Oliver still doesn't answer, but remains transfixed to the game.

'Well, don't play too much. Gran will fix you lunch and I'll be back to make the tea . . . bye then.'

Oliver finally mumbles a farewell, his eyes wide in awe at the beautiful but dark animation playing out before him.

'You got it then.'

Oliver turns round in shock to find his grandmother standing over him looking at the TV. He looks at his left hand still gripping the controls, to find his watch hinting that he's been playing for at least two hours since his mum left.

'Yes Gran, it's just like you said. It's excellent.'

'I see they've left you on your own again.'

'I'm glad this time. I'm already halfway through this.'

'Well done, I knew you could do it. Have you eaten?'

'No.'

'I'll fry us some chips and eggs, and then I'll take over. You can finish it tonight whilst your mum and dad are at the club, and tomorrow, the game really begins.'

Oliver smiles brightly as his grandmother winks mischievously before turning to leave the room.

'Why aren't you ready? You're going to be late for school!'

'Mum, I don't feel well.'

'Oh don't say that. Today of all days! I've got a couple coming for a second showing on a house I've been trying to sell for ages.'

'What's going on?' Bill joins them in the kitchen.

'He says he's not feeling well.'

'He looks okay to me. Get dressed, you'll be fine later.'

'I don't feel well Dad. I've thrown up twice already.'

'Even better, you've got the badness out. Now get upstairs and get ready for school.'

'Maybe we shouldn't force him this time. He does look a bit pale. Honestly Oliver, I can't believe your timing. I'll call your gran. She can look after you. I will not miss work today.'

'Ah you spoil him, that's his only problem. I've told you before; you'll make a wimp out of him.'

Oliver leaves the kitchen and heads slowly upstairs to the sound of his mum and dad arguing over him. A secret smile passes briefly across his face.

Bill is sat in his modern expensive office in a large high street bank, looking for bargain golf clubs on Ebay at his PC. His smartly-dressed secretary walks in carrying an assortment of papers and envelopes.

'Miss Grimshaw, your 9am appointment is waiting, and here's her papers.'

She leaves, quickly followed by the entrance of a beautiful young brunette in hip-hugging flared purple trousers and tight-fitting pink top stretched over a significant boob job. Bill struggles to keep his eyes in check. He finally regains his composure and practically runs round his desk to do his gentlemanly turn with the seat. He resumes his position opposite her. 'Miss Grimshaw, has my secretary offered you a drink?'

'Yes, she has, thank you.'

'Good. You wish to make arrangements for . . . a significant amount of money to be transferred into one of our share options.'

'Yes, but I want you to take care of it personally. You've been highly recommended.'

'Oh have I, by whom?'

'A Robert Henshaw, a friend of our family.'

'Hmm, the name doesn't ring a bell.'

'The transfer of funds is nothing; I would like you to take me to my safety deposit box.'

'I'm happy to, but I'm sure one of my staff can sort that out for you.'

'No. It has to be you. Like I said, you've been highly recommended.'

'Well I'm flattered but . . .'

'Please, there's something locked away which I'm told may upset me. I need a man of your experience to be there.'

'Since you put it that way, I'll be happy to guide you through it.'

'Thank you. That means a lot to us.'

'Mr Dawber, Mrs Dawber, please come in. I hope you're both well?'

They remain silent but smile warmly.

'I believe you want a final look? That's very wise. So I'm going to stay in the back reception room whilst you have a good look round and a chat.'

'No!' they both say in unison. Mary is taken aback.

Mr Dawber continues, 'What we mean is, we'd prefer it if you showed us around. Gave us your opinion if you like.'

Mary is thrown off balance by this request having already mentally put herself in the back reception room with her laptop open. 'As you wish. Shall we start downstairs then?'

The Dawbers turn to each other and smile.

The security guard nods Bill through to the safe area whilst staring at Miss Grimshaw. Bill leads her through a highly-polished corridor with a large metal door at the end. He takes a card from his inside jacket pocket and swipes them in. They enter a large metal room built like a library holding thick metal shelves with built-in metal boxes, and small narrow gaps above each handle. Bill takes Miss Grimshaw to one of the boxes on one of the shelves and inserts a card into the gap. On doing so, a click is heard and the box partly ejects out of the shelf. Bill pulls it off and takes it to a private cubicle nearby. He puts it down on the table. 'There you are. I'll be just over there if you need me.'

'Don't go. I need you right here.'

'It's not for me to see what you have in there.'

'Please, if I should faint or something, I'd rather you be here to catch me.'

'Faint! What have you got in there?'

'All I've been told is that it may upset me, and I'd rather you were by my side.'

'Okay, if it makes you feel better.'

'Thank you.'

Bill takes a step back and Miss Grimshaw opens the lid of the box, her eyes closed as she does so. After a moment she opens them, and as her eyes fix inside its contents, her hands slowly come to her face and she begins to shake her head. She turns round and looks at Bill, her hands covering her mouth and her eyes wide and excited. Unsettled by her behaviour, Bill grabs her shoulders. 'What's wrong?'

Silently she continues to shake her head.

Bill persists, 'What's in there?'

She throws her head back and begins to laugh hysterically. Bill moves her aside, looks in the box . . . and screams.

'As you can see, the garden is huge. It has so much potential, and it's south facing, so no need to say what a bonus that is.'

The Dawbers nod in unison.

'Shall we go upstairs?' Mary leads them back through the kitchen and into the hallway. She thinks she hears whispering and quickly turns round to look at them. She finds them following close behind in single file, looking at her with fixed smiles on their faces. Mary smiles back briefly.

'That's downstairs done. Any questions before we continue?'

They both shake their heads slowly in unison. Mary's sense of unease is growing. She heads up the stairs and onto the landing with one door to the left and three doors to the right, along a wooden corridor with a fourth old and battered door at the end. 'How weird. I don't remember that door being there?'

'We do,' reply the Dawbers, again in unison.

'I must be losing it.'

Mary continues to show them around, first to the bathroom on the left, then the first two rooms along the corridor, giving her usual routine on size, potential and history. She then leads them into the third bedroom. 'Now this room is the largest of the bedrooms and if you look through this door, you may remember we have the ensuite bath . . .'

Mary hears the whispering again, this time like a buzzing in her right ear. She instinctively puts her hand up as if to flick a bee away and turns round to find herself alone. 'Hello, where've you gone?'

She looks around the room in surprise, and then goes back out into the corridor. There is no sign of them. 'Mr Dawber . . . Mrs Dawber?'

Mary's growing feeling of discomfort is now turning to fear. She quickly searches the previous rooms they visited and then looks over the landing rail to the stairs below. They are nowhere in sight. She calls their names again, but the house is silent. Mary finds herself looking at the old battered door at the end of the corridor. She tries and fails to remember where it leads to. 'There's nothing else for it,' she says to herself.

She marches down the corridor towards the door, but the closer she gets, the tighter the knots in her stomach feel. So that by the time her hand reaches for the door handle, it is shaking uncontrollably and Mary is breathing erratically with fear. She pauses, puts her ear to the door, and grabs the handle. She hears whispering coming from inside, but this time she recognises the voices.

'It can't be.'

The door handle she's holding begins to shake violently. She tries to pull her hand away, but is unable to do so. Mary is terrified and confused. 'Hey! What's going on in there?'

She hears hysterical laughter coming from inside and then suddenly, with her hand still stuck to the door, it flings open pulling her inside and shutting her in.

Oliver and his gran are sat on the floor in his bedroom, in front of the TV playing Family Feud. The words *'Congratulations! Do you want to play again?'* appear on the screen. Gran turns to Oliver sat smiling quietly and winks. 'I'll fry us some chips and eggs.'

EXCUSE ME IF I LAUGH
Doreen Roberts

'C'mon Pippa, be a bit daring for a change, nothing's gonna happen. Just watch him like I said, that's all we need do for a couple of days. The clever little git is up to something, I'd like to know why he visits the old girl most afternoons, it'd be fun to get one over on him, smarmy little know all. I think he comes from Planet Prat.'

''S'aright for you to do stupid things Fliss, you haven't got a mum to nag you when you get home late.'

'Stop whinging Pippa, let's have a giggle, it won't hurt just this once. Come on, he's there now, I saw him go in.'

Fliss grabbed her schoolfriend Pippa's arm, dragging her into the direction of the old house where Charlie Porter, the school swot, had just entered. The two girls were now trespassing; they walked stealthily down the broken paved pathway, a-tumble with weeds and overgrown climbing roses entangled with a blue wisteria randomly trailing and disguising an old Victorian pergola.

No sound came from the neglected, once-beautiful dwelling. Fliss pushed Pippa past an entangled gate at the side of the house which led to an equally entangled garden. There were several stone steps up to a patio; miraculously geraniums were still flowering in dilapidated, frost-crazed pots. The leaf fall that had gathered in the pots filled the air with a pleasant but pungent aroma. Leading onto the patio from the house were French windows with tatty, but expensive, lace curtains in a shade of indeterminate cream.

'Look Fliss, Charlie's sipping tea from a posh cup with a plate of choccy biscuits in front of him. He's holding a book.'

'What's he doing with a book? He must be up to something weird. What's the old girl doing?' whispered Pippa.

'Let me get nearer, I can't quite see. Oh bugger that bramble, it scratched my legs. The old girl is laying on the sofa; I think clever git's reading to her. It looks like a worn old bible. Blimey! Quick, run for it, he's seen me.'

The two girls turned, running into pots and brambles, both fell down the stone steps, landing in a noisy heap at the bottom. Charlie Porter came dashing out of the French windows and ran down the steps, staring at the girls he said, 'Hello you two, what are you doing down there? Looks like you need some first aid. Come into the house, Lady Fidelity won't mind, she'll be pleased to have company, but no funny business.'

'What d'yer mean by that?' asked Pippa. 'I've never done much, but Fliss has been caught shoplifting.'

Charlie answered, 'That's what I mean, so don't touch any of the stuff in the house, most of it is valuable, and remember to call her Lady Fidelity.'

'S'pose she trusts you clever clogs.'

'Well yes, I think she does; come in and I'll get some plasters or whatever you need.'

With eager interest, looking swiftly all around them, the girls followed Charlie into the large, sumptuous, but overcrowded very dusty room. There was a faint aroma of vegetables cooking, mixed with damp air from old curtains and cushions, the typical smell of most little used rooms.

Lady Fidelity was a frail, old, shrunken figure, dressed in clothes of charity shop fashion. No doubt they were her clothes from another age.

'Do come in, young ladies, are you badly hurt?'

'No, just a few grazes your ladyship,' Fliss sniggered. 'Can I have a biscuit?' she asked.

'You may. Go into the kitchen and get Charles to open another pack, he knows his way around.'

'Oh blimey, it's Charles is it?' mimicked Pippa. 'Very posh, I must say.'

She went to find Charles in the kitchen, leaving Fliss behind examining the antique trinkets around the room.

She said, 'Very nice, I'm well impressed, but it's not fair for you to have so much and others nothing. What do you say to that Lady Fiddler or whatever yer name is? What's this book that Charles is reading, let's have a look?'

'Oh no, please don't touch the book, it's very precious to me. I've never read the whole of it and Charles, my grandson, comes in when he can to read a little to me. Please don't touch the book my dear, it's irreplaceable you know.'

At that moment, Charlie Porter and Pippa came back with plasters and TCP for wounds, plus a new pack of biscuits.

'C'mon Pippa, there's not much 'ere for us. It's a bit of a let down. The clever git comes here to read to his granny every day.' She walked with disinterest towards the door then laughed, saying, 'I think I'll nick the precious book then the prat will have no need to come here and read.' She picked up the old bible. As she did, its brass clip closed with a click. She pushed Pippa out of the room quickly, turned to grab the packet of chocolate biscuits then shouted, 'Thanks for nothing and don't you tell on us Charlie, or we'll get you.'

The two girls ran off giggling, leaving Charlie Porter and Lady Fidelity to have the last laugh.

She said, 'I suppose we must tell the police Charles; theft is a crime, but I am sure neither of the girls will want to read the whole of the book, even if they could.' The two laughed again.

Later, the two girls were questioned by the police, but denied everything. In due time, the Bible was recovered by the police, its clasp still tightly closed, it was priced £5.00 on a stall at a car boot sale. The man in charge of the stall described Fliss; saying he had given her three pounds for what she said was her family Bible.

The strong arm of the law went to find Fliss. This time she admitted stealing the bible. Both girls were taken to the local police station to face Charlie Porter and Lady Fidelity.

'Blimey Charlie, you look quite normal out of school; s'pose it was you that gave the game away, you little sneak.'

Lady Fidelity answered, 'Oh no it was not, young lady, my grandson had no need to give your game away. I told the police and they were left to do their job. By the way, have you read my precious book yet?'

'No, I couldn't get the rotten thing open, it needs a key; anyway, who wants to read a boring old Bible? So clever clogs really is your grandson? That's something I didn't think of, did you Pippa?'

The silent Pippa shook her head in agreement.

The WPC in charge of the case asked the girls if they had anything to say before Lady Fidelity decided whether or not to bring a charge of theft against Fliss. Pippa remained silent; she was more upset because she had let her friend lead her into something stupid. She shook her head and said meekly, 'Sorry m'Lady.'

Lady Fidelity answered, 'I am sure you mean what you say and I do realise it was not you that stole the book, it was the other girl.' Turning to Fliss she asked, 'What have you got to say for yourself?'

'Don't care much really,' said Fliss. 'It's unfair for you to have so much and others to have nothing; did yer family get all that stuff honestly? Why do you find the need to read the Bible? It won't excuse you from wrong doing.'

Lady Fidelity spoke again, 'Look here young lady, I offer you my book and the key to open it, it is yours; if you promise me that you will read it, or even let my grandson read it to you.'

Fliss grinned and looked towards Charles. She said, 'Wot! 'Ave that creep read the bible to me each day? No chance of that, you must be joking.'

The WPC handed the little brass key to Charles. 'Will you do the honours?' she said.

'That would give me great pleasure,' he said, turning the key in the latch; it clicked. He carefully pulled the brass engraved clasp to release the Bible, which opened with a snap. At least, the cover of a bible opened to reveal some paperback books.

Fliss stared in amazement. 'Good one, Charlie,' she said with her usual snigger. Before her lay a copy of a very popular book about wizards.

Lady Fidelity and Charles laughed. The old lady said, 'I would feel embarrassed if people knew Charles was reading children's stories to me, so I disguised the intriguing books within the cover of an old bible.'

Fliss said, 'I'm gobsmacked! You crafty old bat, you're no better than me, you just cheat in a different way. But you said the book was very precious?'

'It is my dear, it is,' said Lady Fidelity, chuckling. 'I have a whole set of the wizard books and each one is signed by the author, they are worth a mint of money to be given to Charles in return for reading them to me. Just think, a few minutes ago I offered them all to you and you refused. I've had such fun, but the most enjoyable bit is the sight of your mouth hanging wide open, almost hitting the ground. Charles and I pulled a fast one, don't you agree? You are just a petty thief who also trespassed on my land, but I will overlook the incident this time, the joke is on you. Excuse me if I laugh. Come along Charles, don't forget to bring the books. We have time for a few more intriguing chapters before the day ends.'

DEAD CERT
Diane Howard

I had received the black-edged card and a short letter two days ago. I remember looking at the card in disbelief at first, and then, after reading the letter I realised it had to be true. My uncle was my mother's only brother, my mother had passed over a long time ago and I had never really known my uncle, apart from my mother telling me stories of their childhood and how he had always wanted to leave home and join the French Foreign Legion. I believe he had tried to do just that, but they wouldn't have him for some reason or another, and he went on to join a group that rescued animals in Africa. He was the black sheep of the family, and no one seemed to know or care much what he was doing or where he was. We would receive news now and again from foreign climes telling us he was alright and would not be returning to England at any price, he was having a wonderful life and lived it to the full, and the only way he would come home would be in a box!

So, that's the potted version of my family history. I looked at the black-edged card again, something was telling me this had all the hallmarks of being pre-arranged and I hoped with respect it had been pre-paid, because it all looked rather expensive.

The letter told me that the body of my deceased relative was going to be flown home on a chartered aircraft from a small outreach post somewhere near Bulawayo. I was told the precise journey the plane would take, including the stopovers, this was something to do with the pilots having to rest, rather than the state of my relative. I was given the time of arrival and asked if I would be there to sign the relevant paperwork that would release the body for cremation.

This was done a lot easier than what I imagined it was going to be and once I had put pen to paper, the coffin was whisked away. I was then left to return home and wait for the next episode to unravel.

I am now standing outside the crematorium gates, clutching a bouquet of beautiful arum lilies and feeling rather like a loose cannon. It is a wonderful sunny day, one I think the dear departed would have approved of, bearing in mind he preferred the isolation of the great outdoors and the searing sun of the African plains.

I was very early for the service, mainly because I had been extra generous with the time I allowed for the journey, so I walked around the lovely gardens stopping now and again to smell the roses, and admire the obvious handiwork of the gifted gardeners.

I kept checking my watch during all this because I did not want to walk too far afield and have to run back at breakneck speed, arriving only to look like the wreck of the Hesperus.

I was beginning to think it strange I had not seen anyone that looked even a little familiar to me, but it had been a long time since my dear mother had passed away. She had been the mediator and pacifier of the family when she was alive, but with her passing everyone had just slipped into oblivion.

I was still walking around the gardens when I saw a sign that directed me to the chapel. After checking the time again and deciding I really was much too early for the service, I thought I may as well amble back, albeit a different route and go and make my peace with the departed. This 'ambling back' did not take as long as I thought it was going to, and in retrospect those alarm bells should have been ringing, but if they were, I was not listening.

As the little chapel came into view, I had to admire the simplicity of it all, the walls were light grey granite with some beautiful stained glass windows depicting the life of Christ and his disciples. The huge double oak doors were open; as if to beckon one inside and as I ventured in, it was extremely atmospheric as you might expect.

On the floor were laid large uneven flagstones, which had obviously been there for many centuries, and these were relieved every so often by a memorial stone, depicting someone's life. A few of the memorial stones were of those brave men and women who had given their lives for their country in various wars, and a few were of local dignitaries who hadn't.

On the walls were some more commemorative stones and also I was surprised to see some rather unusual tapestries. They must have been very old, owing to the general condition of them, but the work and the skill in being able to make something so beautiful and breathtaking was indeed a work of art, with more than a smattering of passion.

As I walked on through, and my eyes were becoming accustomed to the light or rather the lack of it, I realised that the coffin was already in place just between the two curtains. Not knowing what was expected of me, I went to the end of the coffin and gently laid the lilies that I had been carrying at the feet and spoke a few words. After I had stood there for a few moments I sat down in the front pew and just thought about my uncle and things in general. How life treats you and where the time goes without a cursory glance. Would we have done things differently and would it have made a lot of difference if we had? Why did this man want to leave home and all the people he knew and loved at one time in his life, to lead a nomadic life? Had he had enough? I suddenly felt rather sorry I never really knew my uncle. He could have helped me with my geography 'O' level and possibly history for all I know. There must have been a lot of knowledge and experience in the man after all those years travelling around the African continent.

I felt I was getting maudlin now and one of my legs was getting cramp in it, so I stood up from my sitting position and started to walk around. I ended up where I don't think I should have been. There was a small room just to the left of the organ, well it was more like a large cupboard with a door than a room.

Curiosity has always been my middle name, so it was, I found myself in this cupboard - sorry, small room, and the first thing I did was to switch on the light. In front of me was an array of light switches and a few of these had coloured handles, some had brass nameplates beneath the switch, with a colour engraved into them.

This was too much temptation for my simple mind to handle, and after much - but not too much soul searching, I pressed the blue switch. It was unbelievable, the little chapel became dressed in a swathe of blue light, the curtains were another shade of blue and altogether the little chapel looked like an ice palace, and when I pushed yet another switch, you could hear feint music in the background.

I was in my element; another switch transformed the blue into red. This made the chapel look like a Turkish harem (not the voice of experience, you understand) and I do not think this would have been appreciated by anyone, after all, there is a time and a place for everything as we all know. My next colour was orange, which created a warm glow, but did not lend itself to the vast amount of brass that was present. Too much of this and sunglasses would have had to be worn.

Then we had yellow, and I think my uncle would have approved of this colour. It looked as though we were in the Sahara desert, even the tapestries looked as though they had come out of someone's favourite drinking palace. I felt though it would make my fellow mourners look as if they had contracted yellow jaundice.

Next colour up was purple, now this was very nice, extremely regal-looking and rich. I stayed with this colour and played some canned Bach to accompany it. Very, very soothing, in fact I must have dozed off for a few moments because my only excuse for what happened next was that I was not entirely compos mentis.

As I have explained before, there were an awful lot of switches and one switch was a large red one that didn't have any instructions with it, and it was this switch that was like offering a sweetie to a child. So, the deed was done and the switch was pressed.

All of a sudden the curtains opened and the coffin came forward, and after what seemed a very short while the coffin returned to its position as before. It was then that the curtains started to close. I remember hearing a slight noise, a very slight noise, and then nothing. Absolute zilch.

The coffin, the flowers, had all gone into the ground. What had I done? What could I do?

Run and quickly, this was my first suggestion to myself, but no I couldn't do that. Bach was still playing on as if nothing was untoward, I was sitting in the front pew again, still bathed in a purple light.

I don't know how long I sat there, but I sensed suddenly there were people coming into the small chapel and taking up residence and that I was no longer alone with my thoughts. These people had come for a service and to give thanks for the life of this man, and he was no longer here, the deed had already been done. I think my uncle would have appreciated the funnier side of this situation, but the best is yet to come.

I stood up as if to walk around yet again, and tried to look at some of the faces that were before me, and there were a lot of faces. I never knew my uncle knew so many people or that he had that many relatives still around that would have wanted to pay their last respects.

None of these people looked familiar to me and I would like to have thought at least one or two should have, by the same token no one approached me with an out stretched hand, or smiled a smile with any degree of familiarity.

I checked my watch again nervously as I walked towards the front doors; there was about twenty minutes to go before the start of the service. I was now out in the fresh air wondering whether to go or stay. How can you have a cremation without a body and can you imagine the questions afterwards? But, wait a minute, in the distance is a familiar sight of black limousines and even more familiar is a couple of faces that have removed themselves from the back one. In fact one of the women raises her arm in greeting and beckons me over. I'm not quite sure what is happening here but it would appear there are two little chapels and when I went off for my walk after I first arrived here, I knew that I had walked back another way altogether. Whatever the explanation, I greeted this poor woman as if I had known her all my life, and knew I was talking ten to the dozen about goodness knows what. She asked me if I had brought any flowers, and if so, I could put them on the top of my uncle's coffin along with hers, before it went into the chapel. Flowers, flowers, mine were probably being displayed along with others elsewhere. So, I just explained gently that I had decided to donate some money to the African animal reserve that he loved so much, I looked towards Heaven as I was saying this and offered a silent prayer, in fact I said about three. One for my uncle who I hope would probably see the funny side of all this, one for the person I had despatched earlier and finally, one for all the mourners of both the deceased.

All I hope now is that the chapel is not in purple and the music isn't Bach.

And now, you must excuse me, for I have a funeral to attend.

THE BOX
Jim Crook

The box arrived on a Monday morning, delivered by a bleary-eyed postman in a red van. It wasn't a large box, but it was large enough to be intimidating; not heavy, but heavy enough to carry the weight of the world. Vicky took it from the postman and carried it at arms length, almost as if it contained a bomb. She took it into the hallway and placed it on the coffee table, subconsciously rubbing her hands on her dress as if it was contaminated. Her fears of the box, she told herself, were totally irrational and very unlike her normal behaviour. Why had the arrival of a box, a parcel, a completely innocent object, filled her with such revulsion? She looked at the box; it bore her name: - *Victoria Adams*, the address printed correctly on a white label. Strange, though, there was no postmark, no indication of any forwarding address. Vicky knew she hadn't sent for any package from a catalogue or magazine and her relatives weren't in the habit of sending gifts by post. Her rational side told her to open it, it was, after all, labelled with her name and address; she had every right to see what it contained. But she couldn't; every nerve in her body was rebelling against the instinct to open it. It sat there daring her to reveal its secrets and she felt like Pandora about to release the evils of the world into her living room.

Stepping away from the box, Vicky walked slowly back through the house, towards the kitchen, glancing occasionally back at the box for signs of movement. She had to make a coffee, be rational, convince herself that her behaviour was crazy. How could she, a normal, reasonably intelligent thirty-eight year old woman, with a loving husband, part-time freelance career in advertising, a lovely home, relatives, friends, behave so out of character? How could the arrival of a simple, everyday object conjure up such bizarre feelings? She took the kettle from the hob, made her coffee (stronger than usual - she felt she needed it) and went and sat down in the lounge. Behind her, the coffee table in the hallway with its contents seemed to crave her attention and she glanced round twice for reassurance. Putting down her half-filled cup she stood and turned towards the hallway, telling herself that this was madness; it was only a box, a container for something addressed to her. Maybe it contained a free gift from a promotions firm; a company she had dealt with in her line of work; or even a surprise present (it was not her birthday) from Michael, her husband. She forced herself to take the few steps towards the coffee table, telling herself how stupidly childish she was being. Touching the box-lid tentatively, she slid her fingers gingerly along the Sellotape, thus releasing it and exposing the layer of shredded paper inside. Her hands shaking, she dipped her fingers into the packaging and into the soft, secretive underbelly of the box. At the same moment she jumped, her jangled nerves screaming for release, as the telephone in the lounge demanded her attention.

She almost ran to pick it up, eager to be free of the compulsion to open the box. The words 'sorry, wrong number' and the replacing of the receiver blighted her eager anticipation of the voice being Michael's. She almost felt like ringing Michael at work, for reassurance, both about the parcel and to help her regain her grip on reality, but Michael was a busy man. Their agreement was that she was only to ring him at work (quite often at meetings and endless briefings) in an emergency. He would ring her when he was free. She felt tearful, the ludicrous fears about the box kicking in once more and again she felt the inappropriate terror of the now partly opened box. A box she now couldn't fully open, the moment was gone, the momentum expired. If Michael had been on the other end of the telephone, would she really have shared her irrational fears about the box with him? Michael was a very practical man, a rational thinker, a man who tackled every problem in life head on and he would never have understood this insane situation with the box. No, Vicky had to solve this problem without his help and, she knew only too well, before he came home. She could throw away the box; bury it in the darkness of their cavernous wheelie-bin, safe in the knowledge that within the next two days it would be taken away forever. She would never have to open it, reveal its contents, face whatever it had to show her. Could she do this? Could she behave so stupidly? Until today, the answer would have been a definite 'no'. She had to think, she had to rationalise her fears of the box. When did they start, at the first sight of it? Later, in the hallway? Before its arrival?

Her mind in turmoil, Vicky wandered dreamlike to the kitchen, switching on her kettle once more for a second attempt at a soothing, strong coffee. She couldn't remember the kettle boiling, but seemed to drift from kitchen to lounge with the cup in her hand as if in a trance. The room seemed different, the atmosphere strange and, as she sat down clutching the hot coffee in her welcome hands, a feeling of total numbness overcame her. She felt as if she was floating on air. Was it the coffee? It felt like a hangover, as if she had drunk a succession of double brandies. She closed her eyes and the room seemed to disappear; she had never felt so peaceful, so detached, so unreal. Her eyelids fluttered and she caught a glimpse of her surroundings. She must be dreaming, she felt; this was not her lounge, her house.

She was in her car. Her legs were numb. There was no feeling in her lower body. A warm, sticky, spreading feeling enclosed her head. Blood! She could see it; feel it; taste it! It trickled down her forehead and filled her mouth. She had no recollection of this accident, yes; it must have been an accident. All she could remember was driving to see Michael. He had rung and asked her to pick him up at work. They could go for a meal afterwards, he suggested. The night was wet, it had been raining most of the day and the roads were awash. She hadn't seen the other driver; he had come from out of the darkness. But she had felt the impact of his car, oh God! The noise inside her head! But this was, surely this was weeks ago? At least two weeks ago?

Vicky was aware of herself walking once more towards the coffee table. She looked down at her feet, she felt as if she was gliding over the carpet. She knew where she was going and what she had to do now, the inevitability of it. The box was waiting. She couldn't forestall the moment any longer. The lid was already unfastened; it was so easy now to look inside. She didn't even feel her previous fears, how could she have been so stupid, so untrusting? Placing both hands carefully around the contents, she lifted the single object very precisely out of the box and placed it on the coffee table. It wasn't particularly heavy, just a simple urn, chosen by Michael. The inscription 'Victoria Adams' was engraved on the front. She held it for a moment. No fear, no pain, just realisation.

JOURNEY'S END
T G Bloodworth

The 3.15 from Paddington was on time as it left Kemble. The long tunnel ahead would take it down into the Stroud Valley, headed for Stroud and Gloucester.

Tom knew his fiancée, Mary, would be waiting on Stroud station. He was looking forward to seeing her, having been abroad on business for six weeks. Plans for the wedding had to be finalised, besides which, they had a lot of catching up to do.

Tom was anxious to tell Mary about the job offer he had received. The only snag would mean them living abroad, something perhaps that Mary had not considered.

Meanwhile at Stroud station, Mary was waiting, constantly looking at her watch. The train was reportedly on time, but Mary and quite a few other people were beginning to get impatient.

Another ten minutes elapsed, the train was now late. *Nothing new about that* thought Mary, when suddenly her phone rang. It was Tom, Mary was overjoyed.

'Where are you?' said Tom.

'Still waiting on the platform?' said Mary. 'Where are you?'

'Well,' said Tom, 'the train pulled in a few minutes ago and there is no sign of you.'

'Don't be silly,' said Mary, 'I know the train must be running late!'

Tom replied, but the static made him inaudible. Then Mary's phone went dead.

No one knows what happened to the 3.15 from Paddington that day. The train and its passengers completely disappeared. Investigations went on for many weeks, Mary even reported the strange telephone conversation she had with Tom. Naturally this was dismissed, although a check on Mary's phone did in fact register a call from Tom's mobile. No wreckage was ever found, and none of the passengers ever heard of again.

The train had certainly left Kemble on time, and witnesses were later found, confirming the train entering the tunnel. Many theories were put forward, but no one ever came up with a satisfactory answer. The mystery remain unanswered.

Twenty years later, the London train pulled into Stroud station. Passengers alighted and went about their business. One man however remained on the platform, he seemed anxious and was seen to use a mobile phone. Eventually he approached the ticket office to make some enquiries. Apparently he was due to be met by his fiancée, Mary, as she had failed to meet the train, he wondered if there were any messages, his name was Tom.

A TWIST IN THE TALE
June Witt

Six year old Alice Clarke was the youngest child in a family of nine siblings.

David the eldest was very handsome in a dark, moody way, he had lots of wavy dark hair, he was twenty and was madly in love with Laura. She lived in the same tiny village of Tounbury where the Clarkes lived.

Nineteen year old Colin was a daydreamer and loved to just bury himself in books, anything he could lay his hands on that explained about cars or motorbikes.

Anne came next at eighteen, she was a small, quiet girl with delicate features, she blended into the background and became lost in all the hustle and bustle that was always going on in the Clarke household.

Fourteen year old Adam was a daydreamer with his fair hair and rather big nose and hands, he always seemed awkward and shy.

Ten year old Elizabeth was like a whirlwind going through the house, lots of energy from the moment she opened her big blue eyes at the crack of dawn until she closed them exhausted at night.

George came next in line at eight, he was always getting into trouble, but Alice and George really were so close and best buddies getting into all sorts of scrapes and mischief from running errands for Mum, collecting bread from the bakers and eating half of it before they reached home, to sticking up for each other when they were in trouble at school.

Mum, Anita, often looked at her brood and wondered how they were all so different and the marvel and the headache of bringing them all up safely.

'Will you run an errand for me, Alice?' Anita asked one grey, wet Saturday morning.

'OK,' replied Alice, 'if George can come too.'

'I would like you to take this pot of home-made jam to Mrs Parker.'

Mrs Parker lived on the route from Alice's house to the school and unknown to Mum she was always known as Nosy Parker.

Alice did not like calling there very much because the house was always dirty and Mrs Parker was a large lady who did not look very clean. The house smelt of cats and the hall was littered with newspapers and old cans and bottles. The tiny windowpanes were cracked, dirty and hung with cobwebs. But Alice with George close on her heels knocked at the door, she felt like running away but then it was too late, she heard the shuffling and scraping as the door opened and Mrs Parker came to the door. She looked very grubby, her hair was greasy and not combed, her big, flowered, patterned apron was stained with sweat and food stains. She shuffled on her muddy, frayed slippers, there were patches on her fat legs with veins and purple bruises. Alice felt sorry and afraid at the same time, gave Mrs Parker the jam and left in a hurry.

Next door to Mrs Parker the vicar lived with his pretty housekeeper, then the pink house where the bank manager lived.

The garden of the corner house where two sisters lived was always alive with blossom and colour and Alice loved to look into the garden and imagine fairies and dream castles under the fruit trees that grew in the small orchard.

The summer holidays came and the long days were spent climbing trees, skipping, playing games and chasing each other around the buildings and lanes. Alice often ran errands to Mrs Parker's house and it was always the same. One day when she called she could not get an answer so she ran home to tell Anita. 'Mum, Mum,' she called, 'we cannot make anyone hear at Mrs Parker's.

'Never mind,' said Mum, 'perhaps she is lying down.'

When Alice went to call the next day George said, 'Let's go around the back of the house,' so they did. Alice helped George climb on the dustbin to look in the window. The windows were very grubby and dusty but he called out to Alice, 'Quick, go and fetch Mum, Mrs Parker is lying on the floor.'

Alice fetched Mum and Mum pushed open the back door, the house smelt very stale and Mrs Parker was unconscious. Anita called an ambulance and they sat and waited for the ambulance to arrive.

Alice and George soon became bored and wandered upstairs to look around and see if they could make a good den or find some magic clothes to dress up in. Mum went to find some things for Mrs Parker to take with her to hospital. The upstairs of the house was surprisingly much cleaner as if Mrs Parker had not been upstairs for a long time.

'Perhaps she sleeps in a chair by the fire,' said George.

'Yes, with cats and dogs on her lap to keep her warm,' said Alice.

Alice gently lifted the tiny latch on the old wooden door at the top of the stairs, the door gently moved so that the two of them could peer into the room. There was a very pretty carpet on the floor, it was faded but very pretty, a little bed in the corner of the room covered in a silk flowered blanket. The floor was stacked with boxes and unopened letters and placed under the small window was a little wooden desk. Alice loved it and could not resist going over and sitting at the little desk. It was so delicate and fragile looking with carved flowers and tiny carvings of bees in the flowers. As Alice opened drawers she found a tiny opening at the back of the little cupboard. *Perhaps we should not look in here,* she thought but she felt drawn to it and her fingers just fitted in the tiny gap so she pressed and then the back moved and there was another little cupboard with books and papers and a very old leather photo album. Alice felt very naughty but George and her could not resist as they sat on the dusty floor and looked through the album. There were pictures of a very pretty young Mrs Parker and lots of pictures of family and handsome young men in blazers.

As the two of them became engrossed in the album outside the storm which had been threatening all day broke, with big raindrops splashing on to the dirty panes of glass. They both became engrossed in the book and fascinated by the brown and old photos, they went over the pages and tried to make out who the people were. Soon they were bored and started to play with the wooden box of old papers. Some of the papers were yellowing with age, some had worn along the folds. Then they found a very old, important paper and it fell open just at the moment that Mum decided to come and see what they were doing. She did not mind too much that they had been looking at Mrs Parker's things because they had not damaged anything. When Mum was putting things back she noticed the important piece of paper that the children had been looking at, it was a birth certificate and it was clearly printed that a baby girl, Maise had been born to a Miss Davies, then Anita realised that was Mrs Parker's maiden name and Maise was her baby girl.

When Anita went to see Mrs Parker in hospital she decided not to mention the birth certificate but somehow Mrs Parker who looked all pink and clean in her hospital nightie had a feeling that they had discovered her secret and told the whole story and Mum explained it to Alice and George later over cups of tea and cake how the vicar and Mrs Parker had a baby Maise, and that Maise was the pretty housekeeper to the vicar.

ROSES FOR YOU
Joyce Walker

'Hello dear, how are you? Oh, I shouldn't have asked, you're much the same as ever I suppose, not much changes here, does it?

I haven't seen you for a few weeks, have I? I meant to come, but you know how it is, don't you? Things to do and all that.

Your garden looks a little overgrown, if you remind me I'll weed it before I leave. I know you haven't the strength to do it yourself. Never mind, it comes to all of us in the end.

I saw your Ida the other day. She's made a lovely girl and the children are so well-behaved, better than most, these days. You haven't seen her for a while, I know, but she's so busy and since she moved she doesn't find it easy to get here. You know how it is.

She should make the effort I suppose, once a month at least, it wouldn't hurt, but what with working full time to pay the mortgage. It's just gone up again you know, our Jean's dead worried, she doesn't think she'll be able to keep up the payments and I can't help her. I would if I could but the state doesn't give us much and George's work pension doesn't go far either.

Anyway, I was talking about Ida, wasn't I, working full time? I expect when she's not at work she has to catch up on the housework, but I'm sure she'll come soon, perhaps on your birthday. She does think about you a lot though. We talk about you all the time when we're together.

I haven't seen your David for ages. Not since he started teaching at the Poly' and got that new ladyfriend who lives in Leeds. I suppose he spends all his weekends up there. No offence dear, but there's not much to come home for now, is there?

You know boys, once they get a girlfriend they forget all about their old mum. My Peter was just the same. I haven't seen him since, let me think, it must be five years now.

I get cards and presents, birthday and Christmas, of course, and letters twice a year, though it's usually his wife who writes those. They have two children now, Damion and Tarquin. Honestly, the names they think of these days. I don't know what's happened to the good old ones like John and James. Tarquin, I ask you! Poor little mite. Come to think of it that was the last time I saw them all, at the christening.

They're thinking of emigrating to Australia. If they go, I don't suppose I'll see them at all, though if I start saving now, I might be able to make the trip once before I die.

Oh, I'm sorry I forgot, you find that sort of talk upsetting, but it happens as you well know, it's the only thing in life we can be certain of, dying.

Mary Smith went to a seance the other week, wanted to talk to her Bill, but it wasn't a success. I'm not surprised, they didn't talk much when he was alive, except to shout and swear at each other, she could hardly expect him to come back from the grave. He was probably afraid he'd get another ear bashing. Mind you, she's not given up, she's going again, next week. She wanted me to go with her, but I said you don't need a seance to talk to the dead. I mean if they live in Heaven they should be able to hear you. God's in Heaven, isn't He, and He's supposed to be able to hear everything. Then, maybe we lesser mortals aren't given quite that much freedom, even up there. He might want the ones left behind to have a bit of privacy. I might find out one day, if I don't end up in the other place.

I know what I meant to tell you, we've got new people in your old house. Young couple, they are, very keen to do the place up. It's a bit rundown after standing empty for so long. I talk to them over the fence sometimes and give them a cup of tea while they're working in the garden. It's not the same as the long chats we used to have, of course. I do miss those, but it's nice to see the garden straight again.

The roses are lovely this year, you'd be really pleased with them. I told them all about you and the hours you'd spend in those old gardening gloves of yours with the secateurs, doing the pruning and why I was coming to see you. They gave me these, I said it'd cheer you up. The roses were always your favourites.

How long is it since you've been gone? Three years, three years exactly.

I'll just tidy up a bit and put the roses where you can see them, then I'll be on my way. I want to catch the shops before they close, get a bit of halibut for tea. George does like a bit of fish.

I'll thank the neighbours again for the flowers.

Really, the state this place gets into, I thought the council employed people to look after cemeteries, but it doesn't look as if they bother. Council cutbacks, I suppose. They don't really spend enough on the living, so people like you probably don't count at all. Sad really, because you worked so hard on that garden of yours.

There we are, all neat and tidy, and the roses do look lovely, don't they? I'll come and see you again next week if I can. Perhaps I'll bring you some freesias from the market, unless I can persuade the folks next door to give me some more roses.'

HOMELESS
Trevor Huntington

My God, but it's cold, I thought as I made my way along Firth Street.

The remaining puddles in the gutter had begun to ice up at the edges and the metal grilles of the drains were reflecting the shop lights from their frozen bars. People were moving briskly in the darkening gloom for, although the lights were on in the shops, the streetlights had still to flicker into life. Even as I, too, bent my head forward and strutted, neck into shoulders, I could feel the closeness of passers-by who were keeping one eye out for bargains and the other open to the possibility of a collision.

'Thank goodness it's not raining,' I mused. 'Collars up. Scarves wrapped tight. Glasses steamed up - all we need now is someone to lunge forward and we'll have our eyes poked out.'

I half smiled at my own puerile sense of humour and continued on until I reached the bookshop. *Still open and sadly only one other customer,* I almost said aloud.

'Hello, Richard,' I said, cheerily.

'Come in, Robert. Close the door, keep the heat in,' he said, as he ushered me into the cosy comfort of his somewhat old-fashioned establishment.

'I know you said it would be probably Thursday week but, as I was passing, I thought I'd pop in to er . . .' I left the sentence hanging and, as if he'd read my mind, Richard swung around, hoisted aloft a small parcel and laid it carefully on the desk.

'The miracles of computerised ordering,' he said, a sense of triumphalism in his voice. 'It's only the fourth book I've ordered like this but, I must say, the wholesaler has certainly done everything I asked.'

I thought he might have been on the verge of saying something about the miracles of modern science; but he didn't.

'I suppose you'd like me to pay in a similar fashion?' I again left the question suspended in the environment which was so early twentieth century.

'So kind of you,' Richard replied, semi-mocking, as he pulled forward his previously hidden console for the receipt of credit cards, debit cards etc. 'And any other type of cards so long as I get cash at the end of the day, thank you very much!'

While I examined the books, Richard completed the necessary paperwork and, having signed the no-carbon-required slip, I began to make my farewells.

'The third book will take a little longer, as I said,' Richard said. 'But I'm hoping it'll be here by the end of the week.'

'Many thanks,' I replied, and made for the door, suddenly realising that it was even darker outside and, my coat being unbuttoned, I was not ready for the cold blast which would inevitably hit me.

Our goodbyes became a chorus as I cleared the threshold and I again joined the maelstrom of humankind as we each went our separate ways. Me to the car park; they to, well, wherever they were going, I supposed.

The streetlights were lit now and shadows began to play tricks with my eyes. People turned out to be signboards; litter bins were actually pillar boxes.

There, in the fire exit doorway of the chemist's shop was a pile of rubbish.

You'd think they could have waited until closing time before they put it all out. Someone could trip over it and break their necks, I thought uncharitably.

'Someone's mistaken it for Oxfam next door - they've dumped some jumble ready for the morning, not realising the shop closes early today.'

Sure enough there were at least two plastic refuse bags and a third, somewhat larger, which spilled out its textiled contents over the others.

I still don't know to this very day what made me stop after twenty or so paces. Was it the sleet-specked rain which had begun to fall which got behind my glasses and forced me to seek shelter and clean the lenses? Was it some innate bond which pulled at my soul? The echoes of the 'Big Issue' seller during the earlier part of the day filtered back through my memory. No, it was just a pile of old rags for recycling, surely. Or things for sale in the shop topped off with an old overcoat?

My mind was racing. My heart pounded like the proverbial express train.

I went back to take a closer look. The street seemed to have become deserted; or at least I saw nor heard a soul. Window lights from the shops were less harsh once the shop lights themselves were extinguished. The pedestrian precinct had a cover which arched over all but a central strip at this point and I was able to look ahead clearly towards the bundle.

The rain and sleet were falling on the plastic bags and water ran in rivulets towards the concrete paving slabs. Cold, icy water, onto cold, frozen slabs of unyielding bedrock. Had the bags moved? Were my eyes being deceived once more? Was that an arm in that sleeve?

It did move - and so did I - backwards; repelled by each other's presence. Like the poles of a magnet repel; but we seemed to be invisibly drawn towards each other. I looked down and searched for a hat or similar receptacle in which to place my fifty pence piece. There was nothing. Should I just throw it down? That would be unkind, surely. Like the throwing down of a gauntlet, a challenge; to see if the hand would emerge to steal away the coin into an inner pocket.

A lycra-clad cyclist on a mountain bike hurtled by and, by the light from his intermittently flashing lamp, I could make out the shape of a man who was hunched up in the doorway.

I felt so helpless.

This was beyond my experience. I was once asked what the badge on my lapel represented. I remembered stumbling out the words about it being a sign of a fish and the word fish in Greek was *icthus* and the letters represented Jesus Christ, God's son, saviour. I silently prayed for guidance as to how to proceed. All my instincts said, 'Throw the money and walk purposefully away. Don't look back. Don't run. But walk into the light. To safety'.

Still something compelled me to remain where I stood. Perhaps I should use my mobile phone to get help? Was this an emergency? Do I ask for police, fire or ambulance? 999 seemed so over-the-top for this occurrence. He wasn't doing any damage. He wasn't trapped and, although cold and wet, he hadn't had an accident so far as I could tell.

What was the number for non-emergencies?

Was there a shelter for the homeless in the town?

I felt so helpless.

For no apparent reason a hymn from years ago came back to me: 'When I needed a neighbour, were you there, were you there? When I needed a neighbour, were you there?' I felt like Gene Kelly, singing in the rain! It didn't take a biblical scholar to remind me of what I should do; nor a theologian to remind me of my Christian duty but, well, that's all theoretical, isn't it? It's what happens to other people. And there's the good old Salvation Army to come along and feed them soup and bread and give them a blanket; and Crisis at Christmas, and . . .

The bonds which had bound the two of us together had been made of a single thread of a spider's web, but it manacled us to each other as titanium-hardened steel. Nothing could move us from each other's proximity.

The man - for it was a man - had several weeks of growth to his beard. He was dishevelled but he had the look of a man who had taken care of himself; perhaps ex-army? I couldn't tell, or even guess at his height, but about six feet would be about right. I thought he was gaunt, but how old? I'd read stories of forty year olds who were homeless and they looked as if they were sixty plus. This man looked that, or even older, old enough to be my father. And the coat; ex-army by the look of it. I noticed that there'd once been sergeant's stripes on the sleeve and another badge too; an epaulette hung down limply, a slight river of water dripping from it onto the elbow. There was a movement again from the doorway but this time I stood my ground, trying to focus on the face as it moved into the light from the bodycare advertisement adjacent to it. I looked at it and saw a picture of myself; someone I'd seen years ago when I too had sported a beard; much neater then, of course, neatly trimmed and short. Too much trouble otherwise. Trivial thoughts at such a time as this. I looked again and saw how much I'd aged; how much I'd forgotten amongst all the flotsam and jetsam of my humdrum life; all my self-importance compared to the real hardships of my fellow men, my kinsmen, my family.

My eyes, though wet with rain, pricked with the saltiness of my tears as, arms outstretched, we reached towards each other. I said the only word I could find. 'Dad?'

THE EVENING MEAL
Dennis Marshall

'What are you doing, darling?' he said, going into the room for a CD that he wished to play while frying some chicken nuggets that he had spiced, herbed and started to frizzle in the wok.

'Writing,' she said, without looking up.

'Do you know, I nearly guessed that on seeing the pen in your hand. Your shapely, soft, slender, sweet-scented hand,' he oozed teasingly.

'Shut up! or else you'll have be writing gibberish!' she ordered.

'Yes miss, sorry miss, of course, miss!' he pretended school boy like, seeking her pardon.

'But while you're here; what do you want?' she asked still writing.

'The recipe book, you know, the one Jean gave you for Christmas. It's got something in it I just needed to check!'

'Well look for it! You don't need me to tell you where it is. I'm busy!'

'So I see, but I spoke because I thought it rude to come into a room where my darling was working, ferret about, then leave, without moving my lips!'

She stopped writing. She clamped her pen rather vigorously down on the table top, but it rolled onto the floor.

'There, look what you've made me do!' she accused.

'Hey! Hold on a second. You did that. I didn't ask you to throw your pen onto the floor. Besides that's the one I gave you!'

'No, it isn't. The last one you gave me was a cheap biro! Remember? No, confess!'

'Yes, now I do recollect; you are right because I didn't want to break into twenty pounds.'

'See how easily you make false accusations,' she affirmed, putting her papers to rights.

'Hold on, now, a minute!' he implored, 'you stopped whatever it is you are doing, and then accuse me of interrupting you. I simply came in here to find something, and that something you have removed from the kitchen and left it around somewhere in here. Must have been Monday night when your fricassee of rabbit seemed to bolt from its burrow!'

'Oh! Shut up! You go on about little things that don't matter a cuss! You are a nuisance. Don't you know I'm trying to get a poem ready for a magazine. I should have been more strong-willed on Sunday and not have allowed you to drag me all the way across the common on the pretext that it was what I needed, and what I ought to do. It wasn't! I am healthy enough, and, now I'm coming to crisis point about finishing on time!' She leaned over to pick up her pen and her other elbow deranged her sheets and some slid cheekily onto the floor. 'Damn!' she exploded, 'now look what you've made me do!'

'Oh, I think I'll just quietly get supper.' He paused to pick up the book. 'As you appear to be rather busy now, I guess you don't need an interruption, so I'll go.' He closed the door with a gentle click. Although he heard her raise her voice as he left, he returned to the kitchen. The words of Dylan Thomas came to his mind as the mixture of interweaving scents flew to his nose. 'The world is never the same once a good poem has been added to it.'

His short walk made him reflective. *No,* he thought, *I won't be selfish, I will do enough for her. She's tired, has been over-doing things,* whereupon he added three small new potatoes to the saucepan, threw in some sliced carrots, and into the wok he arranged some more broccoli and sliced green beans.

She's always on about feeding the brute, he thought to himself, *so I'll show her some brutes have a soul, a forgiving, even-tempered nature that she will adore - especially when the smells from the cooking sizzle under her door and permeate her nostrils.*

The kitchen door suddenly opened. 'Something burning in here?' she said, adding, 'you've got that burner on full, no wonder the hall's full of blue smoke. Open the vent, clumsy!'

'Oh, how nice of you to come promptly,' he said. 'I appreciate your coming in to have a quiet chat before we eat; adds such a pleasant pre-meal atmosphere!'

'It's a wonder you could see it's me through all these fumes,' she added.

'My darling, it was your delightful voice that signalled you were near.'

She chose to ignore his gently delivered sarcasm.

'Why haven't you warmed the plates?' she queried.

'Er, I was just about to do that when you came in,' he fibbed.

'Hum! Sherlock Holmes would have noticed they're still up in the rack,' she observed tersely, adding, 'and what are we going to eat with?' He did admit it was one of his failings, forgetting to place the cutlery until laden plates were on the table.

'Thought we'd eat in the kitchen tonight, dear, as I didn't want to disturb you again, rattling dishes and suchlike!'

'I'll give you credit for checking the recipe!' she said, noting the book open upon the table, then suddenly throwing her arms around him she gave him a big hug and a prolonged kiss, saying, 'Do you know, I do love a man who's so thorough!'

CASE CLOSED
Kathleen Townsley

She lay quietly watching the butterflies weave amongst the flowers, too shocked to move, her brain was numb, yet she felt calm lying there in the meadow, not even noticing the blood spreading across her dress, why she was there her brain refused to acknowledge.

'Gypsy come here,' the man called, but the dog continued to bark loudly, 'so much for dog training,' he said. 'Gypsy come, come here girl.' As he approached the dog he saw a hand, pale with red nail varnish, nearing the hand he realised it was not nail varnish but blood. It seemed an age before the police arrived yet he knew it was only a matter of minutes, the ambulance followed close behind. He had remained sitting by the girl, only moving when the paramedics pushed him aside, a police officer spoke to him, but after no response asked another officer to take the priest home.

He must have fallen asleep for he awoke with a start, when he sat upright it was to find Gypsy looking at him and whimpering, that was the first of the many nightmares he had before peace came upon him. Sitting upright he slid off the couch onto the floor and wrapped his arms around Gypsy's neck giving her a big hug, 'Sorry girl,' he said, 'did I frighten you? Just a bad dream girl.' She remained by his side, finally after ruffling her ears, she followed her master towards the kitchen, when he reached down for her dish, all thoughts of the day left her head, all she could see was the dish on the work top and her tummy rumbled.

The following morning after a very restless night, he made his way to the police station, soon he was signing his statement, he asked how the young lady was, and was told she was critical, due to the loss of blood. The officer patted his shoulder and said, 'There was nothing you could have done sir, do not blame yourself.'

The priest rose from his chair and walked towards the door, 'Would you please keep me informed with regards to the child.' The officer nodded and showed the man out of the station. The investigation continued, the officer in charge knew the priest, he was one of his parishioners, yet he still did a thorough background search, well, as far back as the previous two years, the priest only being in the parish that length of time. He knew the old adage of the finder being the villain would not be proven in this scenario, yet it had to be done, the results were as he expected, squeaky clean.

They turned their attention to the young woman's boyfriend; one week into the investigation the young woman died, it had now turned into a murder hunt. Evidence was building against the boyfriend, they had quarrelled openly in the local pub, where her boyfriend had accused her of seeing another man, he was known to be jealous of his girlfriend and very protective, yet everyone said she adored him and would never look at another man, he had been known to strike her, many times.

The officer came to realise Mr Justly was a spoilt, arrogant young man, adored by his father and mother, who could see no wrong in their son, they had hired the best solicitor in the country to defend the young man but the evidence still mounted. The boyfriend was sitting once again in the interview room, his solicitor by his side, the officer said, 'It appears Mr Justly that following your argument in the Hare and Hounds that evening, your girlfriend Sandra was seen to leave the premises in great distress, yourself close behind. A witness said you drove away in your car at great speed, without consideration to other drivers or pedestrians who were themselves approaching the Hare and Hounds, one lady was almost run over by yourself in your haste to leave the premises, therefore we have to assume you either drove out of the car park with Sandra beside you, or you followed her.'

The young man stood up, pushing his chair over as he did and shouted at the officer, 'How many times do I have to tell you, I went home, I never followed her, I have never chased any woman, and I never will, can you not get that through your thick skull?' His solicitor stood and placing a hand on the young man's arm asked him to sit, the young man knocked the solicitor's hand off his arm and turning round said, 'How dare you touch me, you are being paid handsomely to talk to these numskulls, yet you, ask me to sit down, I would be better off without you.' Turning once again to the officers he said, 'I am sick of repeating myself, I did not kill my girlfriend, she did anything I asked, and if not, there was always others waiting in the wings, I suggest you talk to them.' Facing his solicitor he said, 'Now you get me away from here or my father will find someone who can,' and with that he lifted his chair off the floor and sat down refusing to say another word.

The young man still refused to speak. After advising Mr Justly that he was still under caution, the officer said, 'Mr Justly we now have the forensic results from your car, which you admit to driving that night. A large amount of blood was found.'

The solicitor immediately interrupted the officer to say, 'My client has explained this, Sandra had a nosebleed on the way to the Hare and Hound's . . .'

'Secondly, dirt on the tyres has been found which puts your car in the area of Wishing Meadow, thirdly, a coat, which was lying on the back seat of the car, which you identified as yours.'

Again his solicitor interrupted, 'That too was explained, he placed his coat over her knees to stop the blood from staining her dress.'

The officer continued, 'This was found to have a large amount of Sandra's blood, over the whole front of your coat.' The officer waited, when no further interruptions were forthcoming he continued, 'Your car was seen in the early hours of the morning on the road that leads away from Wishing Meadow, by another witness who has stated that once again in your haste you almost run him over.'

Again the solicitor interrupted, 'My client has already stated, that following the argument with Sandra he drove around the district for several hours then he visited one of his ex girlfriends, where he spent the night, I understand you have spoken to this lady and she has verified my client's story.'

'That is correct,' said the officer, 'but she could only say in her statement that following sex, Mr Justly left, and according to the young lady it was around 2am, we asked her several times and she adamant on the time. As your parents were away from the evening of the fourth of August, we cannot verify the second part of the statement, where, and I quote, 'after leaving my ex girlfriend's house I went home to bed', unquote.' Before the solicitor could interrupt again the officer continued, 'Therefore that invalidates what he stated next, that he did not rise till after noon on the fifth of August, as no one can testify to this, I ask again, where were you on the fifth of August, specifically between the early hours of 2 and 7am?' The young man refused to answer and just looked at the officer with disgust. After a slight pause the officer continued, 'According to Sandra's parents, they were not expecting her home that evening, she had told them she was staying at your house. Following a search of your house, a knife was found hidden in the garage.'

Then the solicitor interrupted, 'That could have been put there by anyone.'

The officer continued, 'The knife also had Sandra's blood on the blade and handle, therefore today at 3pm, and in the presence of your solicitor I formally charge you with the murder of Sandra Worthing on August fifth.'

The young man jumped up from his chair and began shouting and hurling abuse, his solicitor could not control the outburst and as the man walked towards the officers with murder in his eyes, the door burst open and two constables entered to restrain the young man, but not before he had taken a swing at their superior, and finding contact had burst the officer's nose.

The man was taken from the interview room kicking and screaming and placed in a cell, he was heard screaming revenge on the officer in charge.

Father Reaper had just returned from his morning walk with Gypsy when the doorbell rang, the same officer was waiting at the door, he could tell by his face that all was not well, inviting him in to the kitchen, the officer said, 'I am sorry to tell you sir, but the young lady died this morning, we have charged a man today with her murder.'

'It will be my pleasure to see whoever did that to the young child, put in jail and the key thrown away,' said the priest.

The officer thought, *I would not call her a child, but I suppose to a priest she is one of God's children.*

When the officer had gone, he went over to his church to begin confession. That night he had the recurring nightmare, he was driving a car when a little girl ran out in front of him, who was now continuing to walk across the road, he called out, as she turned to look at him, the car hit her, tossing her high in the air, that's when he awoke, in a cold sweat. A few weeks later the papers were full of the arrest of Mr Justly, the only son of a wealthy businessman, charged with the murder of his girlfriend, Sandra.

The morning arrived for the priest to give his evidence, he again broke down and the judge had kindly offered the priest a recess, which Father Reaper declined, for he could not rest till all was finished and justice gained. Leaving the court the reporters surrounded him, but a kind constable soon had him safely in his car. That night the nightmare returned, only this time, he stopped, climbed from his car, called Cindy and she skipped over to him, lifting her up he swung her round, placed her in the passenger seat, and drove away, when he awoke the following morning he felt at peace.

The headlines greeted him the following morning, *Guilty,* Mr Justly given a life sentence, Father Reaper smiled. Following breakfast he drove to a little churchyard, and made his way to the family plot. 'Hello Cindy, you can rest in peace now, I did it Mum and Dad, I kept my promise to you both, the man who killed our Cindy is rotting in prison, his girlfriend who was also in the car, is no longer walking this Earth. This is goodbye, you will all remain in my heart forever.'

Later that evening his thoughts turned to the first time he met Sandra, when she had attended confession, not only had they got away with his sister's hit and run, due to his besotted parents and girlfriend, Mr Justly had evaded justice in two further cases. Following the best night's sleep he had had in a long, long time, he rose early, after checking all was packed, he placed the keys to the house on the kitchen table for collection by the incoming priest. Father Reaper sat on the suitcase, pressed the locks into position, 'There Gypsy,' he said, 'case closed.'

THE GOOD SAMARITAN
Peter C Isgar

In a split-second of blind panic I nearly grabbed the gun and threw it out of the window, but the wailing, ever-nearing sirens made me stop. I looked down at the body and watched as the blood crept ever closer across the floor; almost as a last ditch effort to hold on to someone and grasp at life. I kept telling myself, *Look innocent, you've done nothing wrong; you came in too late and found the body.* Like most people in the block, I had flown out of my chair on hearing the shot, and living only across the hall was first to arrive. I had touched nothing; not even the body to check for a pulse. It annoyed me that I was too scared of both a deathly reaction and any implication it might suggest. I knelt down beside him and stretched out my hand, keeping as far away as possible without losing my balance. Luckily his head was turned away so his face was hidden. Although having no first aid training god knows what I would have done if he had stirred! I put my fingers down on his neck; for some reason I expected him to feel cold, I don't know why because he'd only been there a few minutes; there was nothing.

The sound of heavy boots on the stairs, amid shouts of, 'Keep back, stay out of the way!' made me take a step back from the body and await their arrival. Again I tried to maintain a degree of control; my heart was pounding, almost echoing the oncoming footsteps. It seemed an age before they burst into the room with guns raised and pointed at me. Immediately on request I dropped to the floor.

'I have no weapons!' I shouted. 'I found him . . . I *found* him . . . I didn't kill him!' I knew they had to make certain and secure the situation but I was not prepared for their force - foolish of me I guess.

After they'd checked me thoroughly I was allowed to get up. Legs of jelly and violent shaking however, sent me straight back to my knees. One officer, an older man with a kindly face, helped me to my feet and guided me towards the chair. I sat, head in hands, trying to compose myself. I remember thinking how much noise and trampling there was and wondered if they were not disturbing evidence. The room then cleared as another man and a woman entered; the detectives I presumed. I suddenly realised how guilty I must have looked, slumped in the chair, shaking. They stopped and stood in the corner of the room, whispering to each other. Both were dressed in suits; the man, middle-aged and not really fitting his very well; the woman, quite a bit younger and much better styled, appeared to be the more senior of the two. From their expressions I guessed they were talking about me, I strained my ears to hear but the commotion was too loud.

I decided it might give a better impression if I approached them. As I rose from my chair, avoiding the blood, which now covered most of the carpet, they began to move toward me. We met in the centre of the room, just above the head of the body; I glanced down and shuddered at the expression on his face and the already drained complexion. I had to turn away quickly, choking back the vomit forcing its way to my throat; the male detective grabbed my arm and prevented me from falling. With a deep and gravely voice he muttered something about it not getting any easier the more you see. From over my shoulder someone offered a glass of water, which I eagerly grasped, spilling most of it as I did so. It might have been paranoia but I got the impression the female detective was not very sympathetic; she had a look of distrust about her, hard and cold - traits that probably instigated her seemingly early rise through the ranks.

After introducing themselves - he was Detective Constable Jarvis, she Detective Sergeant Moore - Jarvis suggested we go across to my apartment for a bit of peace and quiet. As we entered through the already open door, I picked up the chair I'd knocked over on my way out. I asked the detectives to make themselves at home and offered tea or coffee. Jarvis accepted but Moore declined. It occurred to me as I was making it, how civilised it had all become; calling me 'Sir', drinking tea and coffee, sitting on the sofa; well Jarvis was, Moore just prowled, scowling at pictures and ornaments. I tried to imagine the questions awaiting me and suddenly realised I must be their main suspect. Although still shaken from the earlier events, this sent a new fear through me. My mind raced, I nearly dropped the kettle, scalding myself as some of the water spilled onto my hand. I desperately tried to conceal the cry of pain; I needed to maintain a calm demeanour. I placed a tea towel over the red area and walked into the lounge with the tray.

'What were you watching?' The words came like a dart, straight to the centre of my chest, puncturing, deflating. She stood looking at me, waiting for a response.

'What?' I replied, breathlessly.

'The television was on when we came in; what were you watching?'

Regaining my wits, I realised her attempt to deliberately unnerve me. 'I . . . er . . . I can't remember, some sort of DIY programme I think.' Pathetic. Mission accomplished as far as Moore was concerned.

'But I thought you said you were watching TV, when you heard the shot. It's not that long ago!'

'Yes, but rather a lot has happened in a short space of time. You might be used to seeing corpses lying in a pool of blood, but I'm not!' As I handed Jarvis his coffee, the tea towel slipped off my hand. I quickly grabbed it and winced as I replaced it. I know Jarvis saw, so I was a little confused when he didn't mention it. Perhaps this was the routine; Moore was the hard-nosed one, making you off-guard and nervous, whilst he sat quietly taking it all in, assessing the situation, checking for that piece of information which didn't ring true or the pause before a plausible response.

'Who is the woman in this picture?' Again cold, hard and to the point.

'That's my wife, well ex-wife . . .'

'Left you, has she?'

'No Detective Sergeant, she's dead. She died in a car accident three months ago!'

'Sorry . . . hazard of the job sometimes.' Not even the slightest hint of remorse or embarrassment at her *faux pas*. 'I remember now. I knew I'd seen you somewhere before,' these words were also fired straight to the point but came in a much softer, less confrontational way, yet still with just as much impact. 'Some of our lads dealt with the accident, you had to come to the station to collect some of your wife's belongings.'

'I'm sorry, I'm afraid I don't remember you.' I walked over to the TV and switched it off, it was distracting me, and I couldn't concentrate on what was going on.

An eerie silence filled the room; rumblings could still be heard across the hall, one of the neighbours a couple of doors down was still crying, various officers were shouting orders at people. It all seemed to compound the quiet in our room and accentuate the noise elsewhere.

'I . . .'

'What was your first thought when you heard the shot?' There she goes again!

'What? I don't remember thinking, I just jumped out of my chair, knocked it over as you saw and ran across the hall.'

'How did you get in?'

'The door was open and I . . .'

'Wide open or just unlocked? Weren't you scared the killer might still be there? He could have shot you!'

'It was ajar, I didn't thi . . .'

'Did you see anyone, either in here or running away?'

'Well no I . . .'

'You see, if you ran in there straightaway, as you say you did . . . I don't understand how you didn't see anyone. Do you understand what I'm saying?' She rattled off the questions faster than I could answer, she wasn't really wanting me to answer, she had already formed her own opinion - I was the killer!

'If you give me a chance to answer I might be able to help you! As I said, I fell over the chair, knocking it over, so that must have delayed me getting across the hall, giving the killer time to escape. I don't remember being scared, I just reacted . . .'

'Regular Good Samaritan aren't you!' she smirked sarcastically.

'I don't like your tone; you're not giving me any chance to answer your questions. How do you expect to find out what happened if you don't listen?'

'Because, I don't believe you.'

I couldn't understand why she didn't believe me; I'd gone in there to help. 'Why! Where is your evidence?'

She said nothing, she turned her head up from the sympathy card, replaced it on the shelf and smiled at me; for the first time she showed an emotion and smiled at me.

Jarvis, who had been flicking through a magazine, also raised his head and looked across at her, as if she'd given a secret signal. 'What were you doing when our officers arrived? One of the PCs said you were leaning over the body.' His questions, although direct, never appeared as intrusive; they were enquired, matter-of-fact.

'I was trying to check for a pulse, I thou . . .'

'Trying to check for a pulse! Wasn't it a bit late for that, you'd been in the room five minutes by then!' she interrupted.

'I know, I was scared.'

'Oh, *now* you were scared!' Sarcasm certainly seemed to be her speciality!

'Like I said before I'm not used to being around corpses!' I almost gained comfort in her sarcasm; it indicated to me they were not getting anywhere. The sarcasm was meant to incite, to provoke an outburst.

Jarvis slid his large frame forward on his seat and put his cup on the table, 'What have you done to your hand? It looks like it could use a better bandage than a tea towel.'

He'd obviously kept this piece of information for long enough.

'I spilt some boiling water on it whilst making the drinks.'

'No, I mean the burn on the palm of your hand, not the back. It looks like it has something welded to it, something rubber.'

'It's just a flap of skin. I must have caught it when I fell over the chair.'

'No, it's not is it? You see while you were making the drinks, one of the forensic guys came in with these, he'd found them stuffed into the pocket of the victim.' He held up a pair of latex gloves, 'This one looks to have melted in the palm and would seem to match the position of that 'flap of skin' on your hand! It's all very well wearing gloves to prevent fingerprints, but it's as well to remember that gun barrels can get very hot.'

I froze, my heart pounding, mouth dry.

'I've been sitting here thinking about the accident that killed your wife. No one could understand how or why the car veered off in that manner, it wasn't logical. Then, as I was flicking through your electronics magazine, it occurred to me that it might be possible to install a remote control system to the car; with the car being so badly destroyed in the explosion and the device being so small, it would be easy enough to overlook. I then remembered that the car your wife was driving was in fact registered to the gentleman lying face down in a pool of blood!'

'I think it's about time we took this conversation down to the station, don't you?'

INFORMATION

We hope you have enjoyed reading this book - and that you will continue to enjoy it in the coming years.

If you are interested in becoming a New Fiction author then drop us a line, or give us a call, and we'll send you a free information pack.

Alternatively if you would like to order further copies of this book or any of our other titles, then please give us a call or log onto our website at www.forwardpress.co.uk

New Fiction Information
Remus House
Coltsfoot Drive
Peterborough
PE2 9JX
(01733) 898101